THIS DARING JOURNEY

THE MOUNTAIN SERIES ~ BOOK 11

MISTY M. BELLER

Misty M. Beller
BOOKS

Unless otherwise indicated, all Scripture quotations are taken from the Holy Bible, Kings James Version.

ISBN-13 Trade Paperback: 978-0-9997012-8-7

ISBN-13 Large Print Paperback: 978-1-954810-32-7

ISBN-13 Casebound Hardback: 978-1-954810-33-4

To my baby sis, Elena.
You've been a gift from God since the very beginning. I'm so thankful you're my sister!

A man's heart plans his way,
*But the L*ORD* directs his steps.*

Proverbs 19:6 (NKJV)

CHAPTER 1

"What hornet's nest have I stepped into now?"
~ Samuel

LATE AUGUST, 1869
NEAR FORT HAMILTON, ALBERTA, CANADA

A shot ripped through the air, and Samuel Grant ducked down in his saddle. A reflexive action, because the rifle hadn't been aimed at him.

At least, he didn't think so.

Still, the thud of his pulse accelerated. He must be nearing Henry Clark's cabin along the Belly River. The man he'd been sent to find. Maybe Clark was hunting.

Samuel straightened and cupped a hand around his mouth to sound his presence. But another voice broke through before he could call out.

"Woman, quit yer fire and we'll not hurt you." A deep, tobacco-roughened tone yelled somewhere in the woods ahead.

The men at the fort had said Clark built a cabin out here by the river for his wife. Was she being accosted by intruders? Where was Clark?

Reaching for his Hawken rifle, Samuel slid from his gelding as soundlessly as he could. If Henry Clark or his family were in trouble, surely they'd appreciate help. Another blast echoed as he fastened his horse to a tree. This shot sounded nearer. Maybe it had come from where the man's voice had originated.

He gave the animal a pat, then turned his focus to the danger, creeping from tree to tree.

Another boom. This one's reverberation was more like the first gunshot he'd heard. Not only had it come from the same location, but it sounded like the same model of gun. "I said leave." The woman's voice was muffled by trees and distance, but he noticed something of an accent. Slight. "You do not hear English?" Her tone held a mocking quality now. "How about French." She let loose a melodic string of words Samuel couldn't comprehend. That must be her native tongue, as easily as it flowed.

The man hiding in the woods started to speak again, but the woman's voice rang out, growing in pitch and covering whatever he meant to say.

"Or perhaps you don't understand French either. Must I speak the language of the *dirty redskin* for you to hear me?" The way she spat the label made it clear she disliked the ugly moniker.

Then she spoke in a high-low cadence that caught Samuel's breath. He couldn't understand a word—if they were meant to be words—but each syllable rang with fluid motion. Only a native speaker could be so comfortable piecing those sounds together. Was she Indian then?

He crept closer, moving toward her instead of to the right where the man had to be standing. Another rifle shot brought him up short.

"Did that help you understand, dirty white man? None of my people would act as you have. And now I say again, *leave this place.*"

This woman had more spunk than a starving dog fighting for fresh meat. Could she be Clark's wife? How far had the man gone to hunt? Surely, he'd come to his woman's defense if he were close by.

"You can spout your fancy language all day. It won't change what we came to do." The gravelly voice again. It held just enough leer to make Samuel's gut churn. *We* meant there was more than one man trying to advance on her. "We've got enough fellas to quiet you down for a long time, but things'll go better if you put your gun on the ground."

Samuel shifted his direction toward the men again, tuning his senses to pick-up on any sound they made. As he crept forward, both warring parties fell silent.

He kept his steps as noiseless as possible, walking on the balls of his feet and straining for any sign of movement through the trees. When he caught a flash of brown, approximately the color of the buckskins most of the men at the fort had worn, he ducked behind a sturdy tree. He needed to get closer so he'd have a good shot, but he'd have to wait until the men were thoroughly distracted.

A faint rustle sounded from the direction of the attackers, then half a second later, another shot exploded. A man screamed, filling the air with curses and names no woman should hear, much less be called.

When his screaming settled to muttering, she called, "There's more where that came from."

Samuel peeked around the tree. The men were shifting, maybe bringing back the injured man. This was Samuel's chance.

He darted forward to hide behind another tree. He was closer with fewer branches encumbering his view. He could see four men. Rangy mountain men, just like all the others he'd seen at the fort. Crimson smeared the shoulder of one, whom the others gathered around.

They were talking in low murmurs so Samuel couldn't make out the words. But they must have reached a consensus, for the three uninjured men straightened and raised their rifles. They looked to be planning an attack. If he didn't act now, he might lose his opportunity.

Positioning his gun, he aimed down the sight at the tree just above one man's head. *Lord, let this do the trick.*

He squeezed the trigger, and the bullet surged toward its target in a deafening blast and a cloud of gunpowder.

Another shout. More cursing as the men turned to find this new source of danger.

"Get down." The one with the most gray in his full beard motioned the others toward a fallen log. The wounded man limped slower than the others, clutching his shoulder.

"That won't help you any." Samuel filled his voice with as much confidence as he could muster. "I have half a dozen men hiding with rifles aimed at you. And five more circling around to your rear."

As he motioned toward the trees behind the attackers, he could see the tops of their heads spinning to search.

He pushed his advantage. "You'll obey the lady's orders and leave here, or I'll tell my men to pick you off one by one. It won't take more than four shots, you can be sure."

The older fellow spoke. "We've got no trouble with you. That woman's husband sold us this place. We've come to collect."

Samuel barely bit back a growl. "By running her out of her house? Or did you plan to make her part of the bargain? Either way, you're not collecting today. We'll let you get your horses and ride away, but if one of you so much as looks back, I'll give the sign for my men to let loose. Clear?"

Gray Beard raised his head a little, scanning the area. Samuel worked hard not to flinch, not to show his hand.

Just then his gelding whinnied from the trees behind him. Other horses answered, probably those belonging to these men. The cacophony filled the woods.

The ruckus must have appeared to give truth to his bluff, for Gray Beard raised his hands, then eased up from behind the log. "Don't shoot. We'll leave. Like I said, we've no fight with you and your men."

"All four of you stand up, then drop your rifles right there." He aimed his gun at their leader, but kept his gaze circling all four of them. He wasn't naïve enough to think these were the only weapons the villains possessed, but he was counting on their fear of his greater numbers to keep them from circling back with other guns.

When they'd laid their rifles down, he said, "Now march toward your horses and mount up. Once you're on, I'll give you to the count of twenty before I give my men the nod to start shooting. I suggest you be out of range by then."

"We'll be gone." The men marched toward the shifting animals he could just see through the branches. Gray Beard had a stiff set to his shoulders, as though not a bit happy with being forced to leave his prize. The injured man stumbled, unsteady. Thankfully, one of the others helped him mount.

When they were all in the saddle, he gave them one last reminder. "I start counting now."

Gray Beard sent an annoyed scowl back his direction, then signaled his horse forward, the others following close on his animal's tail.

In less than a minute, the crashing of the animals' hooves through the woods died away. Eerie silence took over the area.

Samuel eased out a breath. Now he had to figure out where Henry Clark was, and why his wife had been left alone to defend herself.

And he had to make sure he didn't get himself shot in the process.

～

*M*oriah Clark angled her face so she could see better through the peephole between cabin logs, straining to catch any motion in the trees at the edge of the clearing. She could hear the occasional hum of male voices, but no movement. Were they spreading out to approach her from all sides? That's what she would have done from the start if she'd been planning the attack. Thankfully these men weren't so strategic.

And thankfully, she'd sensed something was wrong before the first man stepped from the trees. Before she met Henry, she would have assumed that instinct was her ancestors' spirits warning her. Now, she could direct her thanks to the proper source.

Thank you, Lord. And please give me wisdom to know how to fend them off.

A rustling in the cradle behind her spread tension through her shoulders. Then a soft murmur. *Not now, Lord. Please.*

She sent a glance back as the blanket shifted, and a tiny hand rose up from the cloth. Another mew sounded. Cherry wouldn't be put off much longer. Moriah's own body told her how long it had been since her daughter's last meal.

She turned back to the peephole to scan the woods again. The crash of steps sounded in the trees, too heavy for men. Horses? Were more strangers coming? Surely these intruders weren't leaving of their own accord. Maybe she should send another shot their way.

Her daughter let out a cry, the warning kind that always preceded a full-blown wail. If she didn't at least pick-up the babe, the men would hear and know she was more vulnerable than she pretended. She couldn't shoot attackers and nurse an infant at the same time. So far, she'd been able to keep Cherry a secret from the rest of the world, and she couldn't let that change now. Both their lives would be in even greater danger.

With a final scan revealing no more motion in the trees, she turned from the lookout position and laid her gun on the table, then strode toward her baby girl. She slid her hands under the bundle of blankets swaddling the little body, then scooped Cherry up and tucked her close. "It's all right, honey. We're safe."

Cherry nuzzled Moriah's neck, seeking out her long-awaited meal. The feel of her tiny, trusting daughter was almost enough to distract her from the danger outside. Or at least make her want to hide away and pretend everything in the world was as sweet and innocent as this new life.

But she couldn't let her guard down. Cherry depended on her mother to be strong, to protect her from evil men. Her daughter had no idea yet about the ways of the world. Especially in this territory where half-Peigan women who married white men were considered nothing more than a commodity. Worth a handful of horses, if she kept her mouth shut and filled her husband's belly.

Turning, she held her daughter close and moved back toward the peephole. She couldn't shoot the rifle with Cherry in her arms, but it was quiet outside. Maybe the men had left. Was that too much to hope for? God could perform miracles, so maybe He'd answered this prayer. *Finally*.

Cherry's nuzzling became insistent as Moriah peered through the hole to the world outside. The baby banged her little mouth against Moriah's neck to show her frustration. "It's all right, sweet one. Wait a minute longer." She bounced to soothe the babe even as she tried to focus on the trees.

Something moved out there. A blue cloth shifted among the branches, then a man stepped from the woods.

Her body tensed. Should she lay Cherry down so she could shoot at him? She had to. If he advanced much closer, he could charge the cabin and barge in before she could react.

But he stopped. Only a few yards away from the trees, he halted, his gun held loosely in both hands.

"Ma'am. I ran those good-for-nothings off, and I'm not here to hurt you." His voice rang loud in the clearing, deep and commanding. It held a civilized edge, unlike the men who'd made three attempts now to take over her cabin. Was this another of their tactics?

He spoke again. "My name is Samuel Grant. I've come to see your husband, Henry Clark. I assume this is his place. I'm a friend of his sister, Rachel. She sent me with a letter for him."

The words seemed foreign as she tried to draw them in. Henry's sister? Had Rachel heard of her brother's death?

Moriah's heart thudded hard in her chest. That wasn't possible, since she'd been careful not to let anyone know of his passing these last six months. She'd known the harassment would start as soon as men from the fort realized a woman lived alone in this well-built cabin.

Cherry shifted again in her arms, rooting into Moriah's neck as she renewed her search for nourishment. She grunted her dissatisfaction at being thwarted for so long.

"Ma'am. Are you kin to Henry Clark?" The man outside shifted and seemed to be growing impatient.

If he really was a friend of Henry's sister, she owed it to Rachel to let her know of her brother's death. Henry had been so fond of the sister he hadn't seen in over a dozen years. He'd read her letters for weeks after receiving each one. In fact, he'd been using those missives to teach Moriah to read English.

Before the hunting trip that changed everything. Her heart squeezed at the reminder.

"Ma'am?" The man was peering toward the cabin as though he thought maybe she'd slipped out the back door. He might come investigate if she didn't say something soon.

Cherry let out a complaint, the kind of cry that came just before the true wails. She wouldn't be silenced much longer.

Moriah had to get rid of this man.

CHAPTER 2

"Trusting has never come easy, and with good reason. This time, no less than any other."
~Moriah

*M*oriah pressed her mouth close to the peephole and raised her voice loud enough for the stranger to hear. "Henry is my husband. You can leave the letter where you stand and be on your way. Thank you for delivering it." *Lord, let him think that sufficient.*

The man didn't move to obey, just stood there. His head tilted slightly. "Actually, Miz Rachel is nearby. About three days' ride away. She's planning to get married again and was hoping her brother would come for the ceremony."

A flare of hope warred with the fear inside Moriah. And when Cherry loosed a louder cry, desperation joined in the mix.

The man must have heard the babe, for he straightened. "Is everything all right in there, ma'am?"

She had to take care of her daughter, but she couldn't leave this man standing in the yard for the next half hour, wondering what was happening inside. He seemed to truly be a friend of Rachel's, but maybe she should ask a few questions to be sure.

Leaning closer to the opening, she asked, "Where is Rachel staying? Does she have anyone with her?" They'd received her last short note saying her husband had been killed in a gambling fight, but Henry had assumed she'd stay at her home in Missouri and keep working the farm. Her son, Andy, should be old enough to help her now.

"My brother and I met Miz Rachel and Andy at Fort Benton, then traveled north with them and another man. My brother's the one she's planning to marry, and they're waiting at my sister's house in a little valley tucked in the mountains."

He knew Andy's name, so that was a good sign. But there was one more thing she needed to know before she placed any trust in him. "Why did she leave her home?"

The man cocked his head again. "She was coming north to see her brother—your husband."

A pang hit Moriah's chest, landing squarely in the ache that still lingered even six months after Henry's passing. Rachel's journey had been for nothing.

But the man continued. "I got the feeling that, after her husband died, she wanted to start over. Someplace new."

Maybe Rachel could still have that fresh start in this country. Especially if she'd found a man worthy of her.

Cherry pressed harder on Moriah's neck, crying out with an insistence that wouldn't be denied. It was time Moriah show herself and her daughter to this man. Let him know she'd need a few minutes before dealing with him further.

Bouncing a bit to distract her babe, she moved to the cabin door and elbowed the brace aside. She blew a strand of hair from her face, then pushed the door open and stepped outside.

She had to blink in the sharp daylight, so much brighter than the dim shadows in the cabin. She'd run out of oil for the lanterns, so she'd put them away, although she never would have lit them in daytime anyway.

The man standing across the clearing removed his hat, drawing her focus to him and the gentle grin spreading across his face. "I wondered what that fussing was. Now I see."

Cherry wouldn't stop fretting now. She'd be caterwauling soon. Moriah patted her back and continued bouncing. "I need to tend to the babe for a few minutes. Can I trust you to stay put until I return?" She'd be watching him, of course.

He nodded, still gripping his hat in one hand and his rifle in the other. "Yes, ma'am. Do you mind if I step back in the woods and get my horse? Then I'll come right back to this spot and wait for you."

If he was as honest as he sounded, she'd thank God all day. But she knew better than to trust a white man. She'd seen too many of them sink into vile depravities.

She turned and stepped back inside the cabin, then placed the brace on the door and took up her position by the peephole. Her rifle lay within reach, but she'd need both hands to care for Cherry.

She unbundled the babe and changed the wet cloth. She couldn't help the warmth that flowed through her every time she tended her tiny daughter. "You're finally going to eat, my sweet one. Patience is always rewarded." If only that was true for her. It seemed like she'd been holed up in this cabin forever, waiting for things to get better. Yet, the danger seemed to grow with each day.

Cherry paused in her squirming to stare up at Moriah with Henry's wide eyes. At just three weeks old, everything about her seemed tiny except those eyes. Moriah leaned close and pressed a kiss to the soft skin of her daughter's cheek. While she was close, she took a second to breathe in the sweet baby scent. Nothing could be more wonderful.

But then she forced herself to straighten and peek through the hole in the cabin wall. No sign of the man. Hopefully he was still gathering his horse and not stealing around to approach from the other side.

She turned back to her daughter. "Let's get your belly full so we can send him on his way."

~

 $\mathcal{I}$ t seemed to take an hour for Mrs. Clark to come back out of the cabin, but after Samuel collected his horse, he returned to the spot where he'd promised to stand and didn't stray. This woman clearly wasn't afraid to shoot that rifle of hers, and he now knew the root of her spunk—fear. Or whatever it was that made a female bear so ferocious as she protected her cubs.

He hadn't been able to see the baby well over the distance, but he'd seen enough to know the infant was tiny. A newborn.

Where was Henry? They must need food awfully bad for him to leave his family vulnerable for a hunting trip. That had to be where he'd gone. Samuel couldn't think of another reason why the man would leave them alone.

At last, the door creaked open, and Mrs. Clark stepped out again. He had to blink to take in what he was seeing. She wore something strapped on her back—something bulky—and carried a bowl in one hand and a rifle in the other.

She walked toward him, and he wanted to meet her partway, but he didn't dare. He wanted her to know she could trust him.

As she neared, he couldn't take his eyes off her, even to eye the bowl of something steamy she carried. Her dark braid and dusky coloring reminded him of the Indian women he'd seen in the camps they passed on the way north. Yet her hair wasn't coal black but coffee brown. Her eyes were lighter still, like coffee with a bit of milk lacing the cup. She wore a shirtwaist and skirt just like any other white woman. Could she have blood from both races running inside her? Regardless, Henry had found himself a pretty wife.

Speaking of Henry, Samuel held out the letter. "Here's the note from Rachel. She didn't say her brother was married, but I assume she won't mind if you read it before your husband gets back."

The woman took the note and flicked her gaze to the paper before looking back at him, as though she didn't trust him to stay put while she turned her focus to the missive.

"I think it basically says that she's only a few days' ride away and she's getting married," he said. "She'd really like her brother to be there for the wedding. I'm sure she'd love to meet you and the child, too." He nodded toward the cabin where the baby must be. "If you're up to travel, that is."

She raised her chin, and he waited for whatever fiery response she planned to offer. But instead, she handed the bowl toward him. "Eat. You must be hungry after coming so far."

The smell of the stew had been teasing his belly, and the sight of hearty chunks of meat in warm broth made his mouth water. She'd even added a spoon. He glanced at her expression once more—just to make sure she wouldn't change her mind and dump the hot liquid on him.

Her face was impassive. Completely void of expression, although she hadn't lost the regal bearing of her shoulders nor the weary creases edging her eyes. Caring for a newborn added those lines to women's faces. He'd seen it before among their neighbors in Yorkville. A lifetime ago.

Taking the bowl, he nodded his appreciation. "I am hungry. Thank you."

He scooped a bite to his mouth, letting the warmth soothe his insides even before his tongue picked out the flavors. The meat tasted like venison, but she'd added spices or something to enhance what could sometimes be a flavorless meat.

Another bite slid down, even tastier than the first. Although he focused on the soup, he kept an eye on the woman at the edge of his vision. He'd eaten half a dozen spoonfuls before she finally looked down at the letter again, fingering the corners of the envelope. More than half the meal was gone before she slit the wax seal and unfolded the papers.

Her gaze narrowed in concentration as she studied the words. As he scraped the last bite from the bowl, she lowered the letter and returned her focus to him.

He gave her a grin. "This is the best venison stew I've had in ages."

She nodded, her face softening a tiny bit. Then it went rigid again, as though preparing for what she was about to say. "My husband died several months ago. While hunting. Please tell Rachel how sad I am to share that news."

The words slammed into him like an ax blade hacking a tree, and he swayed a bit from the impact. "He's...dead?" His gaze scanned to the cabin again. *Several months ago.* Before the baby was born? Henry had never known his child. Even worse, had this woman endured childbirth alone? Surely there was a doctor or another woman in the area she'd called. Maybe her mother.

But why had she been left alone to care for the baby and manage all the other work required to survive in this wilderness? That infant had looked so tiny, Mrs. Clark likely hadn't yet recovered from the birth.

He turned his focus back to her. "I'm more sorry than I can say for your loss. I'll hate to break the news to Rachel, too." His mind spun in a new direction. "Maybe you'd like to come meet her? I know she'd appreciate the chance to know her brother's wife." His gaze slipped back toward the cabin. "And your little one, too. Is it a boy or girl?"

"A daughter." She turned slightly, revealing the structure on her back.

It was something like a satchel, and he almost jumped when he saw the blinking eyes near the top.

The baby. Swaddled in layers of blankets so only her tiny face peeked out, Henry's daughter hung from her mother's back. He thought of the stories he'd heard of Indian papooses. He'd never seen one before now.

His chuckle slipped out before he could stop it, and the woman spun back to him, concealing her child behind her.

She looked as though she thought he planned to attack the child. He had to explain his laugh. "I didn't realize she was hanging there."

Her face still held suspicion, so he tried to sober his expression. "What's her name?"

"I call her Cherry." Again, the woman's expression softened a little.

It was easy to see she loved her daughter, and no wonder, with the babe's adorable innocence.

"Cherry?" An unusual name, but this seemed like an unusual pair. "I like it. Sounds sweet. Has she been healthy so far?"

Mrs. Clark's chin bobbed. "So far."

He eased out a breath, forcing his mind back to the more consequential topic. "I'd like to escort you to your husband's sister. She and the rest of our family would be pleased to see you. There are kids and babies aplenty, so lots of mamas happy to help out." Traveling with a newborn wouldn't be easy, but he surely couldn't leave this woman to fend for herself. Was she even recovered from childbirth yet? Maybe they'd need to wait a few weeks.

She raised her chin, all regal defiance. "I thank her for the offer, but I will go back to my people. I have been waiting only for the babe to gain a few weeks. The time is almost here."

She had family then. *Thank you, Lord.* Did she mean Indians or whites? Not that it mattered. As long as she had people around to help her, he'd not worry. "How far away is your family?"

She turned her gaze westward. "About three days' ride to the west and slightly north." Then she brought her gaze back around and leveled it on him. "A Piegan camp in the mountains."

He nodded. "I can help you get there on my way back. I'm headed southwest, but it's probably not more than a day or two out of my way."

She eyed him as though waiting for something else. Some other response. Did she expect a reaction about her Indian ancestry? Or maybe she was debating within herself whether to accept his offer.

She would probably balk at it, as independent as she seemed to be. But she'd need help on the trail with an infant. Especially being only a few weeks out from the birth, she surely didn't have her strength back. There was no way he would send them on their merry way alone. If he did, he'd be launching her and the babe to certain torture, maybe even death.

Still, he waited for her to speak next. Better to know the level of her resistance.

"It's not a hard journey. I will travel alone." She spoke calmly. Resolutely. Then she nodded toward the smaller of the two buildings, the one connected to a corral. "You and your horse may stay the night in the barn before returning to your people in the morning."

So, she was dismissing him. Telling him he'd better be gone by first light. At least this was a kinder send-off than she'd given the others. *Leave this place* in three languages.

Indeed, this was quite a woman. Yet he wouldn't be swayed by her strength. She needed help, and he'd be patient until she was ready to accept it.

CHAPTER 3

*"My commission is clear. How I'm to accomplish it, though, is still a bit
murky."*
~ Samuel

Moriah warred within herself all night. Each time
Cherry pulled her from exhausted sleep for a nursing,
her mind worked through Grant's offer. She wasn't naïve enough to
think traveling across country with a three-week-old would be an
easy thing. It was hard enough to manage here in the cabin, shielded
from the elements with the dwindling supply of logs and food she'd
stocked up before the babe came.

But she could do it. She had to.

When there was no better choice, you simply did what had to be
done.

But now she did have another choice. Could she trust Samuel
Grant? Just because he was a friend of her husband's sister didn't
make him trustworthy enough to share a campfire with. She didn't
sense a bad spirit in him, but trusting a white man was no small thing.

As her mother had learned the hardest way of all.

Cherry awakened just before the blush of dawn lightened the horizon, so Moriah mixed up gruel for herself and the man outside, and steeped a pot of coffee the way Henry had liked it. If her visitor left this morning like she'd back-handedly suggested, she'd consider it God's leading and worry no more.

But if he stayed... She didn't know what she'd do if he stayed. Maybe wait a few days so she could get a better reading of his character.

When there was enough light to see by, she made her morning trek to the river with Cherry strapped to her back, following the path through the trees bordering the bank. This had been the perfect place for a home, near the water but with the fringe of woods giving them privacy from those traveling the river.

The men who'd pestered her these past weeks knew it too. They'd surely move in the very day she left, just like the squatters they were.

On her return to the cabin, sounds of activity drifted from the barn. Her guest must be stirring. He'd surely had a cold night without a fire to heat by, so he would appreciate the steaming food and coffee. Maybe she should invite him in to warm himself by her hearth. But she wasn't quite ready to share the tiny cabin with another man, even for a few minutes.

Cherry gurgled in her cradleboard as they made their way to the barn. With a bowl in one hand and a tin mug in the other, she could only manage a tap on the barn door with her toe.

Seconds later, rustling sounded louder inside, then the door pushed open. The soft morning light shone on the man, bundled in a winter coat, his hair ruffled as if he'd combed his fingers through it moments before. A bit of dried grass clung to the scruff of his short beard.

And when his gaze rested on her, his mouth curved in a smile that would warm her if she let it. His eyes held the same kindness Henry's had, although the men's appearances were different in almost every other way. Henry's stocky frame and flaxen hair were nothing like the tall, lean build and darker features of this man.

She'd always loved the way Henry's eyes made her feel safe. She was reminded of that safety from the way Samuel Grant looked at her now.

She extended the bowl and cup. "Gruel and coffee. They should help warm you."

He accepted the offerings. "Thanks." His voice still had a sleep-roughened quality. He raised the cup to his mouth, and his eyes drifted shut as he took a long sip of the brew. As he lowered the mug, his lids opened and he exhaled a long sigh. "That's real good. Just what I needed."

She nodded. How exactly was she to respond to that?

He leaned against the door post and nodded toward the cradle-board. "How's our little one today?"

Our? She glanced over her shoulder. "She's well. Up early as usual."

"Does she stay warm enough bundled like that?"

Something she often worried about. She turned so he could see the baby. "We don't stay out long when it's cold, but she seems to like being snuggled where she can see the world."

"Hey, there, Cherry." His voice softened. "You do like to see things, don't you?"

He looked back at Moriah. "I don't know that I've ever seen a person so little. How old is she?"

There couldn't be any harm in answering that question. He knew the babe was young and hadn't yet taken advantage of her weakened state. "Three weeks yesterday."

His eyes widened a tiny bit as he looked back to Cherry. "My, but you're a sweet young lady." When he spoke to her daughter, his voice took on a gentleness that most men wouldn't show.

The sound brought a burn to her throat. Would Henry have been like that? Probably. He'd been hardworking and no-nonsense, but never had he shown himself cruel. He would have loved his daughter.

She straightened, forcing the thoughts that had no bearing on the present from her mind. "If you get too cold, knock on the cabin door, and you can warm yourself by my fire."

Had she really said that? She shouldn't let herself fall prey to distraction again, or who knew what she'd offer up?

Turning, she retreated back into the house. To safety.

~

Samuel took another sip of coffee as the cabin door closed behind Mrs. Clark and the baby. He'd been pretty sure she had a softer side under that stone armor she wore, and this breakfast proved it.

And she'd even offered up her cabin should he be on the verge of freezing to death. Of course, she'd looked as if she wanted to clamp a hand over her mouth after she said the words, but they'd still slipped out.

He gave in to his grin as he stepped back inside the barn. At least this structure kept the wind out.

How long before she finally gave in and allowed him to escort her to her family? A few days? A week? For that matter, how long before she would be ready to travel? That could be several weeks still, if it had only been three since her childbirth.

And that baby was *so tiny*. Surely, she needed to grow more before they exposed her to the harshness of nights on the trail. He'd best hunker down for a few weeks' stay at least. Maybe he could rig a branch shelter in the yard to sleep in so he could have a campfire at night.

He'd need to chop more wood unless Mrs. Clark had a stash hidden. The dwindling pile alongside the cabin wouldn't last long. How was she doing with food? He had only a few days' supply for himself, and he'd need to do some hunting to supplement that. If her husband had been gone several months, she probably needed more too.

His next few days would be busy.

As soon as the sun cleared away the fog, he took the ax into the woods and chopped the first felled pine he found that wasn't rotten.

He'd just worked up a light sweat when the little hairs at the back of his neck tingled. He'd laid his rifle a few steps away, but his hunting knife hung from his belt. Should he lunge for his gun or ease around and see who was watching? It might simply be Mrs. Clark, not the men from yesterday come back for vengeance.

He shifted just enough so he could see out of the corner of his eye without alerting the person that he knew of their presence.

A flash of blue caught his gaze, the same dark blue as the blouse Mrs. Clark had been wearing that morning. He turned fully, taking in the sight of her squared off about a dozen strides away and framed by trees.

The babe cradled in her arms did nothing to soften the glare marking her stony face. She looked as if he were hiding in the woods shooting at her like those cads yesterday.

He raised his brows and summoned his most gentlemanly tone. "Can I help you?"

"What are you doing?" Her words emerged clipped. Angry.

He glanced back at the tree. Had she been saving it for something? "I was cutting firewood. I wasn't sure how long it'd be before we head out, and there's not much left stacked beside your cabin." He turned a rueful gaze on her. "I was also thinking I might camp out in the open and have a fire at night, if you don't mind."

He held his breath, trying to find some hint in her expressionless face of what she was thinking. Was she angry because she still didn't want him to accompany her to her family? Maybe she'd thought he'd pack up and ride away this morning.

Finally, the line of her jaw eased. The movement was slight, but he'd been watching close enough to see it. "The next time you intend to raise a ruckus in the woods, please alert me before you begin."

Understanding washed over him like a pail of icy river water. He'd frightened her. She must have thought her attackers had returned. He had all the thoughtfulness and sensitivity of a mountain goat, charging his way through his work without a thought to what she might think of his racket.

He took a step forward. "I'm sorry, ma'am. I didn't even think about how much noise I'd be making. I just knew we'd need more wood, but it didn't occur to me to speak to you first." And now he sounded like a selfish boar.

She held her regal stance for another moment, then said, "We won't need much wood. I'll be ready to leave in another few days."

The tightness inside him eased. *A few days.* Now, he had a time frame to work with, not the uncertainty he'd been fumbling with before. He set the ax head on the ground. "Take as long as you need. I don't want you to feel rushed because of supplies. I'd thought to go hunting later today. I'm not sure how you're set for food, but I only brought enough for a few days."

She regarded him with a steadiness that was almost unnerving. "I have traps set, ready for me to check them." She hadn't answered his question exactly. It was clear she was still trying to be self-reliant.

He'd let her do what she was able, but he'd also make sure they both had food. "If I can bring in a deer, it sounds like we'll be set."

She returned his nod, then turned and walked back toward the cabin—her tread soundless, even through the brittle leaves of the forest floor. She must have learned that ability from her Peigan family.

~

*I*t was time to leave this place. Moriah sat wearily the next morning, nursing her half-asleep babe. Her body was growing stronger with each day. More time would be nice, but her spirit urged her to go. Perhaps danger was closing in.

She'd let Mr. Grant know her decision to allow him to accompany her, then take this day to pack. They could be on the trail the next morning. As much as she dreaded the trip, she was miserable here, holed up in this lonely cabin. The place smelled of desperation. Of fear. The long months after Henry's death had been fraught with worry, but nothing like the night of Cherry's birth. Pain beyond anything she'd imagined. Blood everywhere. The terror of fearing her babe had already died, destroyed by Moriah's ineptness. Relief had come so powerfully that tears had streamed down her face when Cherry raised her first cry.

Though the fear had abated after the babe's birth, it crept back more with each day as Moriah had struggled with each new aspect of motherhood.

Being the sole provider and protector and nurturer for her fragile daughter was pressing her to the edge of her sanity.

The sooner she left this place, the sooner she would have the help of her people. Maybe then she could find the peace she craved. Henry had said God was the source of serenity. And she'd believed that while her husband lived. She'd prayed for peace and felt it in some measure. But Henry's death had stripped away whatever peace she'd gained through her new faith.

Surrounded by people she trusted, perhaps she could find the connection to God she'd been working so hard to develop. Even though her people didn't know Him, she could share what she'd learned.

As daylight streaked the eastern sky, she peered through the peephole toward the little camp Grant had made beside the barn. He'd placed his fire far enough from the building that she didn't worry about the structure catching flame, but it probably helped protect him from the wind.

Besides, she'd be losing the cabin and the land to the squatters the moment she left. It shouldn't matter what happened to the buildings. Except she could still remember working alongside Henry as they built both structures. The task had formed a sort of unity between them that she missed.

Outside, Mr. Grant was adding logs to the low flame. He must have done that several times during the night for there to be any fire still burning now. She left her peephole, poured coffee, and scooped out a bowl of gruel. This meal could get tiresome, but at least it would fill him with warmth.

She needed to make pemmican today for their food on the trail. So much to do, even though she didn't plan to pack much. The horses needed to be brought in from the pasture and checked over. Perhaps Mr. Grant could help with that. *Lord, please let them still be there.* She'd hidden the animals in a remote area where she didn't think they'd be discovered by the men who'd been harassing her. But there was always a chance.

Cherry lay snuggled in her cradle, her sweet face innocent in sleep. Moriah hadn't put the baby in the cradleboard like she normally did after her first early morning meal. Maybe it would be all right to let her daughter sleep while she took the food out. As long as she didn't dawdle.

Mr. Grant straightened when she stepped outside, then stood and moved forward to meet her partway. "You're a godsend, Mrs. Clark. Thank you for this."

She nodded as he took the dishes. "There's more coffee in the pot on the stove. Knock on the door when you finish this, and I'll refill your cup."

His mouth parted in a grin. "I'll do that. Thanks."

It was a wonder how a little thing like warm coffee and a hot meal could bring out a smile like that.

She turned back toward the house. "I need to get back in to the baby."

"Yes, ma'am. Thanks again."

She'd already stepped inside and fit the brace on its bar to lock the door before she realized she'd forgotten to tell him the most important part.

Tomorrow they'd be leaving. And it couldn't come soon enough.

CHAPTER 4

I am resigned, and the thought of this change fills me with more relief than I should feel. Am I as weak as they once said?

~ Moriah

Samuel stood at the doorstep but couldn't quite bring himself to knock on the cabin door. *She said to come, you weakling.* After two days, she'd finally offered. But he hated the thought of scaring her again, especially not for a mere cup of coffee.

A blast of icy wind blew through him, just as the gusts had done most of the day before. It felt like weeks since he'd been warm. Maybe that coffee would at least keep him from freezing until the sun strengthened a little.

He raised his fist and knocked before he could lose his nerve. "It's me, ma'am. Just come for the rest of that coffee."

Within seconds, a scraping sounded inside. The door cracked open, then moved wider, as though she'd wanted to make sure it truly was him before allowing access.

He held out his cup and couldn't help a sheepish look. "Just wondered if you still had any of that coffee warm?"

Her face softened into what almost looked like a wisp of a smile as she took the tin and turned to the fireplace. Daylight wasn't strong outside, so he could see inside the cabin without trouble. His gaze fell to a rough wooden cradle carved out of a hollowed log. As unique as the piece was, the angelic face inside was what drew his attention. Little Cherry slept peacefully, her mouth puckered in a tiny O. She had slight indentions above her brows as though she was concentrating hard on her dream.

Mrs. Clark approached him with the steaming cup, and he nodded toward the baby. "She's like a little angel." He kept his voice low, barely more than a whisper so he wouldn't wake the child.

She paused for a second to watch her daughter sleep, and he couldn't seem to stop himself from studying the woman out of the corner of his eye. A soft smile eased over her face. "She is. Especially when she's sleeping. I only wish she'd do more of that during the night."

Then she turned back to him, her mouth pressing shut as though she was sorry she'd said something so personal.

He offered a grin to ease her discomfort. "Doesn't sleep through the night yet, huh?"

She shook her head. "She's getting better, but we still have a ways to go."

Then she straightened, her expression changing to her usual serious look. She motioned through the door. "Let's go out so the cold doesn't wake her."

He obliged, his gut tightening as he stepped down the stoop to the ground below. She must have something significant to tell him.

When he turned to face her, she leveled her gaze on him. "I'll be ready to leave out tomorrow morning. Will that suit?"

Tomorrow? When he'd startled her by chopping wood, she'd said she'd be well enough in the next few days, but he'd not expected her to be ready so soon. Could she have everything packed by then?

Still, he nodded. "Tomorrow is fine." He'd accommodate her. "Do you need help packing? I saw three horses in a pasture on the other side of the woods. Should I bring them in?" And perhaps go for a hunt. He'd not made it out to find game yesterday either. One task had turned into another until it had been too late to start.

She looked a little uncertain. "I do need to bring the horses in. I should take care of it, or at least help you. There's a yearling who will tag along if we bring the mares."

Surely he could take this one thing off her shoulders. He gripped the warm mug with both his frozen hands. "I worked on a ranch in California for about three years, so I'm a decent hand with horses. Unless you just want to help, I can bring the mares in on my own."

A flash of relief crossed her face, but it was so quick he might have misread her. "All right. Call for me if you get into trouble with them."

He nodded. "Yes, ma'am. Anything else I can do? I'll go hunting this morning, then see if I can get the meat roasted this afternoon so we can take it with us."

Her gaze lifted to stare out above his head, but her thoughts seemed far away. "That's enough. Thank you." Her tone was almost wistful, and he wasn't entirely sure she was talking to him. Her expression seemed to be locked somewhere distant, or maybe into the past.

He should probably leave her to her thoughts. He had more than enough to do today, so he'd best get started.

Easing backward, he offered a parting nod. "Thanks again for the coffee." Then he turned and walked away.

⁓

*M*oriah was exhausted by the time late afternoon rolled around. The packing of her own things wasn't hard. A few supplies for cooking on the journey, along with the scant remnants of food she had left. Her buckskins to wear when she was back among her people. She only wore the English clothes now because the pliable shirtwaist was easier to manage with nursing.

Most of the things she'd gathered in her life with Henry she wouldn't be able to take with her. His clothes and the items he'd made or purchased for her through the years. She would take his Bible and the letters from his sister he'd been using to teach her to read English.

At first, she'd not wanted this life she and Henry had created together. She'd only agreed to marry him because her grandfather arranged the union. She'd trusted her grandfather, trusted that he would value her safety and happiness more than the goods he would receive in trade for her hand in marriage.

And he'd been right about Henry. Blessedly right.

Her gaze wandered toward the door as she turned the pemmican cakes over in the pan. What was Grant doing out there now? The sun had cleared away the bitter wind by mid-morning, and she'd taken Cherry out to soak in some of the warmth and check their traps. But the man wasn't there. The low brush shelter he'd built was still in place, along with the pack he carried supplies in.

When she'd stepped outside again a few hours later, she'd seen him scraping a deer hide. Thinking of it now, she realized she should offer to roast the meat, especially since she had the better hearth and pan to do so.

After she finished the pemmican, she would ask.

But more than an hour passed before she'd finished her cooking and nursed the now bright-eyed baby. Finally, she bundled her daughter in the fur swaddling she'd stitched and held her against her shoulder. "Shall we go see Mr. Grant?"

Cherry bounced and made an effort to raise her head off Moriah's shoulder, as though showing her excitement. Moriah couldn't help a chuckle. "I know you like him. He seems to like you, too."

She'd been surprised when he showed so much attention to the babe. Indian men usually paid little notice to the youngest members of the tribe, mostly because so many little ones didn't survive their first few years. It was easier to bear the loss if there was not a strong connection with the child.

She tucked Cherry under her chin and breathed in the sweet baby smell. She couldn't imagine not loving this sweet child. Losing her would be too much to even consider. These few weeks they'd spent together had changed Moriah in ways she'd never imagined. This all-consuming love, the determination to build them a happy future. She was so much fuller for the gift of this tiny baby. And definitely more exhausted.

When she pulled open the cabin door, she scanned the edge of the woods before settling her gaze on Samuel Grant. He knelt beside his campfire, and as she neared, she saw the sliced meat sizzling on a spit over the flame.

He turned to face her as she and Cherry approached, and his easy grin made her want to return the welcome. He had a way of settling her nerves. Whether she was worried or afraid or simply exhausted, a conversation with him always seemed to uncoil the knots inside her.

"I was just about to go bring in the horses, now that I have this last bit of meat started roasting." He motioned to the baby. "How are you and Little Bit getting along? Find anything I can help with?"

So he didn't need her help with the meat after all. She almost wanted to have something for him to do nearer the cabin, if only to have him around. She must be starved for human companionship. Before Samuel had arrived, it'd been six months since she'd had a conversation with another soul that didn't involve rifle shots and threats.

Other than Cherry, of course.

Mr. Grant was waiting for a response, brows raised, so she shook her head. "Bringing in the horses is a big help. I thank you."

He wiped his hands on a cloth, then stood. "I'll get to it then."

As he turned to walk away, something inside her squeezed tight, sending desperate words from her mouth before she could stop them. "Would you like to come inside later for the evening meal?"

He paused midstride, easing around to face her. "I'd like that." He seemed to hold his breath, as though waiting for her to change her mind.

Should she pull her words back? He'd proved himself trustworthy thus far, but allowing a man inside the cabin was no small thing. Still, if she planned to travel alongside him and share a campsite, a stronger test of his honor might be a good idea. And since he'd slept in the bitter cold without complaint, the least she could do was offer him a warm meal in a heated cabin.

So she offered a nod. "I've been cooking for our journey, so it will be the same fare we eat for the next few days. But at least it's warm."

His easy grin came again. "Warm. That's the best word I've heard in a long time."

Cherry took that moment to make her presence known, bouncing on Moriah's shoulder with a sweet baby coo. Moriah turned so the little one could see Mr. Grant.

"Hey, there." He stepped nearer and gentled his tone. "Will you be there for the meal, too? I've never seen you this awake."

The babe bounced again, lifting her head off Moriah's shoulder with a jerk, then dropping it back down. Her sweet expression looked for all the world like a grin, although she hadn't offered her first smile yet. Moriah's heart couldn't help but squeeze tight at the innocent happiness of her little daughter.

"I think she likes your voice." Cherry's exuberance must have rubbed off on her. She shouldn't have said that, and now she couldn't quite bring herself to make eye contact with the man.

He chuckled. "I like her too, so it's mutual." He stepped back, finally giving Moriah space to gather her wits. "I'll bring the horses in now. See you shortly."

As he walked away, she eased out the breath that had been building inside her. Why did she seem to lose her good sense around this man? Nerves from being around another person after all these months alone? Maybe. Especially being around a man.

Yet there seemed something different about Samuel Grant and the way he affected her. She'd need to maintain better control around him. Especially as they would spend so much time together these next few days.

After that, he'd be gone forever. And she and Cherry could start a new life—a life she knew well.

And thought she'd never return to. Would her people accept her without concern? Or would they find her too much changed?

～

*O*nce again, Samuel stood at the closed cabin door, preparing to knock. This time he made himself raise a fist and tap without pausing.

The rustle of footsteps sounded inside, then the grating of the brace that held the door tight. Her tread was always so quiet, surely she couldn't be so silent wearing boots. Did she wear women's slippers? He'd seen ladies wearing them in towns back east, but no woman in her right mind would wear silk slippers in this wilderness. Maybe she was simply skilled at softening her step in boots.

She cracked the door enough to confirm it was him, then widened the opening and stepped aside. "Come in."

He stepped inside, and the warmth that met him was almost suffocating—in a delicious way. "Whew, this feels good." He turned to offer a grin of thanks.

She didn't meet his gaze, just closed the door, then approached the little table. She motioned toward the fire. "Warm yourself."

An offer he wouldn't refuse, and he tugged off his gloves as he sauntered toward the healthy blaze. "Where's our little girl tonight?" He realized too late how those words sounded. Cherry wasn't *his* girl, but he was surprised at how quickly fondness for her tiny face was growing within him.

"She's over here." Mrs. Clark motioned toward the floor hidden behind the table. "She's squirming now that she hears you."

The words made it impossible to keep his grin in check as he half-stood to peer over the table. What a sweet little bundle. He'd like to hold the little angel, but he didn't dare ask. Not yet anyway. There might be a time when Mrs. Clark needed an extra set of hands, but he'd have to content himself until she trusted him.

Besides, if he did something wrong or dropped the baby, he'd never forgive himself. Better to smile and talk to her from a distance.

Just now, he stayed by the fire, letting its warmth thaw his aching bones and bring his fingers back to life with a burn. Mrs. Clark dished food onto two tin plates, an appealing meal of some kind of meat in a gravy sauce, with a lumpy, flat, cake-like bread. His mouth watered just watching the food.

"There." She pushed the plates to opposite ends of the table in front of each chair. Then, she looked up at him, possibly for the first time since he'd entered the room. "Ready to eat?" Her voice always held a clear, lilting sound. Just enough of an accent to draw him in.

He nodded, turning his focus to the food again instead of her many charms. "More than ready."

CHAPTER 5

"How she manages with such grace, I'll never know."
~ Samuel

*A*s Samuel sat across from Mrs. Clark, silence settled in the room, illuminating every pop of the fire, every scrape of a chair, every clang of a fork on a plate. Even his breathing. And his chewing.

He should probably find something to say. Anything to draw her attention away from his table manners—or lack thereof. He wasn't sure what she was used to, but he'd never been quite as refined as his ma and big sisters tried to make him.

Before he could swallow the bite in his mouth and find something to say, Cherry came to the rescue. Little grunts and murmurs sounded from the other side of the table, snagging Mrs. Clark's focus. She watched the baby for a long moment, pretty indentions pressing into her brow.

The little noises grew louder, sounding more like real complaints now. Mrs. Clark sent him a look. "It never fails. She always needs something the moment I sit down to eat."

A half-cry sounded, and Mrs. Clark bent down to fiddle with the child. A moment later, she straightened and positioned little Cherry in her arms so she could see Samuel. The babe had a grumpy look on her face that was so cute it made him smile.

"Are you hungry too?" He raised a fork full of the tender meat. "This is good food your mama made."

A half smile touched Mrs. Clark's face. "I don't think she's quite ready for this." She positioned the babe to free one of her hands, then leaned around the little one to eat. She performed the act skillfully, as if she had much practice. He guessed she'd like to eat a meal with both hands for once.

He set his fork down. "Would you like me to hold her while you eat?"

She paused mid-bite, sending a quick glance at him, then to her daughter, then back to meet his gaze. "I'm accustomed to it. You're the guest. Enjoy your food." Then she dropped her focus back to her food, sending a clear message.

He obeyed, taking a few more bites before he ventured another comment. "The horses did fine when I brought them into the barn. They're well-mannered animals."

She raised her gaze to him. "Good." Her look made it seem almost as if she'd forgotten about the animals. That was the way it should be. If he could take the weight of some of her responsibilities, he'd be content.

"Which mare do you normally ride?" This way he could have the horses saddled and ready in the morning.

"The bay. The chestnut is the mother of the yearling. If I tether her behind my saddle, the colt should follow along without trouble."

He nodded. "I hoped as much. My gelding is a friendly sort. Do you mind if I tie the chestnut behind him instead of your mare? That way you can focus on you and the baby without worrying about extra horses."

Her eyes blinked, the only sign his suggestion caught her off guard. "If the animals get along."

"I'll let them get to know each other first, then we'll see how things go."

"Fine." She took another bite, turning her focus back to her food and her daughter.

He let silence settle for another minute as he took in the cabin around them. The place was well-built. Not much by way of furniture, but any man in this territory would be lucky to have the place. Did he dare poke his nose where he didn't belong? But he wouldn't feel right about taking her away without asking.

After swallowing his bite, he motioned around the room. "This is a nice cabin. Do you have it sold to someone who'll come in after you leave?"

She didn't answer right away, just continued chewing, the steady action of her jaw almost painfully methodical. At last she swallowed but didn't lift her focus to his face. "I do not. Those men will be back to take over the place before the fire cools, no doubt, but I'll not take a penny from them. I want nothing of theirs." She almost spat those last words.

He did his best not to flinch away from the venom in her tone. "I can understand the feeling. It just seems like you'd get a decent amount for selling the place. It's up to you, though."

Her jaw hardened. "I only want to go back to my people. I need nothing else."

She must have endured an awful lot to have such anger. The thought pressed hard on his chest.

He couldn't erase her past, but he could protect her from this point on.

oriah pulled the cinch tight on her mare and positioned the stirrup back in place. "Ready, girl?" She patted the thick winter hair on the horse's neck and tightened her hold on the reins as the mare shifted. "I know it's been a while." Too long since she'd ridden either of the horses, but they seemed to have weathered their time in the pasture well. All three were round and wooly with winter coats.

"Want me to hold her while you mount?" Mr. Grant's voice sounded nearer than she'd expected, but she kept herself from reacting.

"I can do it." After all, she'd grown up on horseback. Having the cradleboard on her back would require a shift in balance, but she shouldn't have trouble.

He didn't press the issue, and she managed to climb aboard the mare without much awkwardness. Cherry had already settled into a deep sleep, lulled by the rocking of Moriah's steps throughout the early morning.

The hours of riding ahead of them would probably keep her in that peaceful trance longer than usual before she awoke hungry again.

Mr. Grant mounted his big red gelding and looked at her with raised brows. "All set?"

She sent a final glance toward the cabin, the home Henry had struggled over, the place that had turned from a peaceful home to a warm prison. Now, she just wanted a fresh start.

Squaring her shoulders, she turned back toward Mr. Grant. "I'm ready."

Two hours later, her body made it quite clear how long it had been since she'd ridden horseback for this length. Worse than that, Cherry had awakened and was fussing in the cradleboard, more than ready for her next meal.

She should have positioned her daughter in front, maybe even in a sling so she could nurse as they traveled. If she asked Mr. Grant to stop for the babe to eat every two hours, their trip would take days longer.

Cherry let out another squawl, and the man riding just ahead reined his gelding to the side so she could ride up alongside him. They were in open country with mostly grass and rolling hills except for the trees gathered along the occasional creek they passed.

When she was beside him, he glanced back at Cherry. "Is now a good time to stop and stretch our legs?"

A surge of relief washed through her. At least she didn't have to ask for a halt. Most men would be frustrated at stopping so early in the morning, but he was offering without a hint of displeasure.

She nodded, and in seconds, she'd dismounted and was removing her daughter from the cradleboard. "It's all right, sweet one. You're going to get clean and fed." Once again, the complete dependency of this child pressed down on her. There was no one else to care for her. No one to fight away the men who would have tossed her aside as not worth the trouble while they plundered the things they craved.

She couldn't let herself dwell on what would become of this sweet baby if anything happened to Moriah. She had to stay alive. Had to get them to a better place. The pressure to accomplish it was almost smothering, but she'd bear up under the weight and get them to safety.

She had to.

~

Samuel kept an ear tuned to the woman and child behind him. But he tried not to look at them, as much as he wanted to. Just now, she was humming, the sound barely carrying up to him through the creaking of saddle leather and swishing of grass under the horse's feet. He strained to hear her pretty voice.

His gelding's ears pricked, catching Samuel's attention. On the horizon was another line of trees, but as he stared, several bits of brown separated from the brush.

Men riding toward them. Or at least he assumed they were men. He'd only seen one other woman since leaving his sister's home in the mountains, and she'd been an Indian squaw at the fort.

He glanced back to point out the newcomers to Mrs. Clark, but she'd already seen them.

She met his gaze, her focus intense. "They are white men."

He turned back around to study the figures. All he could see were three specs of brown. He could just make out the bulky outlines that did probably mean they were male. But white? It was impossible to tell the color of their skin from this distance.

He kept his focus on the strangers and spoke loud enough for Mrs. Clark to hear. "How can you tell?"

"The way they sit their horses. No Indian would slouch so."

He almost chuckled. Now that he studied their shape, he could see the truth in her words. He'd not had enough experience with Indians to be so certain of their posture astride a horse, but she clearly had.

The group seemed to be coming straight toward them, which made sense because Fort Hamilton lay to their back. Within a few minutes, the distance between them had closed by half, and Samuel could make out more details of their faces.

He eased his horse slower and to the side so he could speak to Mrs. Clark without his voice carrying. "Do you recognize them?" He glanced at her face.

Her jaw was tight, and she'd tossed a fur over her shoulder, shielding the baby from view. "Maybe." She kept her gaze on the approaching men. "There were so many at the fort, it's hard to remember them all."

"They're not the fellows you were fighting off when I came, are they?" He didn't see Gray Beard among them, but she might have gotten a better look at the others than he had. His gut coiled as her answer was slow in coming.

"I would know them better by their voices."

That didn't ease his worry any. He refocused on the strangers and gave his gelding more rein to move out in front of Mrs. Clark and the baby. She stood out like a shimmering angel in this wilderness of men, but the more he could protect her from their gawking the better.

The three men reined in a few strides away, and the fellow in front tipped his hat up. "Howdy." His gaze slid right past Samuel to the woman behind him, then seemed to hover there. Narrowing.

"Hello." Samuel made the word strong to pull the attention back to himself.

The man swung his focus to Samuel and took him in. "You folks come from the fort?"

"Near there. Is that where you're headed?" He let his gaze travel over all three of them, giving each an equal chance to answer.

But it was the bushy-bearded man in front who responded. "Yep. Got a load o' furs from the Indians." Then his focus shifted back to Mrs. Clark. "Say, aren't you Henry Clark's woman? I knew I'd seen ya before." He darted a quick glance at Samuel. "But this ain't Henry Clark. That's what gave me pause."

His question was clear. Why was she traveling with a man not her husband? Samuel had to bite his tongue not to set the record straight. He wasn't sure how much she wanted to make known. He finally summoned what seemed like a satisfying, yet vague enough, answer. "I'm escorting Mrs. Clark to visit her family, as I'm going that way myself."

The man's head tipped as he studied Samuel. "Her husband passed on?"

"Yes." The word drifted from behind him before Samuel could string together an answer.

All three strangers turned to face her, and Samuel couldn't help but do the same.

She raised her chin and met the eyes of the man who'd been doing the talking. "My husband died on a hunting trip. I am returning to my people."

He'd never seen a woman look so noble. So brave. But he couldn't stop to watch her now. He forced himself to focus on the men, to see their reactions.

The bearded fellow narrowed his beady eyes. "I'm sorry to hear that, ma'am." He didn't sound a bit sorry. He looked from her to Samuel, then back to her. "It's good you'll be around kin again."

Did he think something untoward was happening between the two of them? Samuel should set the man straight.

Before he could speak, though, the stranger straightened and glanced at his two friends. "We'd best be movin' on. Won't be stoppin' tonight 'til we get to the fort."

Maybe it was right that he let it go. Surely neither of them would see these men again. And both he and Mrs. Clark knew their traveling together was strictly for assistance and protection. That was what mattered.

As the men rode off, he slid a glance at Mrs. Clark. She met his gaze with a rueful look. "I'd say my little cabin just found its new owners."

He studied her for signs of anger. "Does that bother you?"

She heaved out a breath. "I suppose I gave it up." Then she glanced down at the mound of sleeping baby hidden under the fur. "We have to put that life behind us."

He'd never met such a strong person. Except maybe Rachel, the woman his brother would be marrying. But Rachel hadn't survived for months on her own, heavy with child. Then given birth to that child, completely alone. Then fought off men who'd planned to take over her home and have their way with her.

No, this woman possessed more strength and gumption than any person he'd ever met, male or female. It was an honor to help her make this journey.

An honor, yes. But something in his gut told him this might turn into more than the simple trip he was hoping for.

CHAPTER 6

"Who would have thought this freedom I craved would be so hard to find?"
~ Moriah

The sun was high in the midday sky when little baby coos and mews drifted from behind Samuel. He glanced back to see the babe stretching in the sling Mrs. Clark had wrapped her in. A tiny fist reached out from the fabric as the coo turned into fussing.

He glanced in front of them. "Looks like there's a creek not far ahead. Shall we stop to eat and rest the horses?"

"That would be good." Her voice hung heavy with relief. Tending an infant on horseback couldn't be easy.

When they reached the spot, he dismounted just in time to hold her mare while she eased down with the baby. "I'll water the horses while you do what you need to with the little angel."

She sent him a look that might have been meant as a smile, but the weary lines and shadows under her eyes took all the cheer from the expression. She'd been bearing under a heavy load far too long.

After he loosened the animals' girths so they could breathe easier, then let each drink its fill, he tied them where they could graze a little. Next, food for the people.

He found his roasted venison and pulled out strips for both Mrs. Clark and him. She'd probably packed better food, but he didn't want to riffle through her things to find it. She was probably as thirsty as he was from the morning in the saddle, so he took his tin cup a little upstream from where the horses had drunk and scooped up the clear water.

Bearing food and drink, he headed back toward Mrs. Clark. But the moment the trees between them thinned enough for him to see her clearly, he froze, then spun away. She sat, leaning against a tree, a blanket draped over the front of her. He wasn't naïve enough to wonder why that blanket covered her and the babe who must be in her arms. Didn't infants fuss because they needed to eat?

His ears burned from the thought of what he'd walked in on, and he moved away, back toward where he'd left the horses.

"It's all right, Mr. Grant."

He paused. She didn't sound angry, nor did she sound nearly as mortified as he was. "I'm sorry, I…" Words fled his mind.

"I'm covered. You may do whatever it is you need."

He inhaled a breath. She was much calmer about this than he was. But then, it was the way of nature, right? A mother nursing her young. Just as God planned things.

He eased back around, careful not to let his gaze wander anywhere near her. "I…was just bringing you something to eat." He kept his focus on the ground in front of him as he carried the food and cup forward. "All I have in my pack is the venison, so I hope it'll do for now."

He set the cup down beside her, and her hand appeared from under the blanket to take the meat.

"Thank you. I am very hungry. And thirsty."

Of course she was. She had to eat and drink for two.

He turned away, having succeeded in not looking at her once. "I'll get more meat. Let me know when you finish that water and I'll fill the cup again."

"Actually, stay for just a minute and you can take the cup now."

He paused while the sounds of drinking drifted up from behind him. Almost as loud as the pounding of his pulse.

"Here. Thank you."

He eased back around and took the cup, his focus grazing her face as he did. She was the same woman he'd ridden beside minutes before, her grateful smile now evident. The drink seemed to have revived her.

He nodded, forcing his racing heartbeat to ease. Forcing himself to act naturally. "I'll get more meat for you."

She nodded. "If you look in the right side of my saddle pack, I've wrapped up some pemmican. That should go well with the venison."

"I'll find it." He turned away and forced himself not to break into a run as he retreated toward the horses. As he went, he sent up a prayer. *God, I think I'm gonna need a different kind of strength than I expected on this trip. Help. Please.*

When he brought the refilled cup and pemmican, he was surprised to find that Mrs. Clark had already finished the large chunk of meat he'd left with her. She surely was eating for two. He'd need to do a better job of making sure she had enough throughout the day.

"Can I bring you anything else?" He was doing better at making eye contact without his ears melting.

She leaned her head back against the tree as she took another sip of the water. "This is wonderful. Thank you. We won't be much longer." She looked exhausted, but not as desperately so as she had when they'd first dismounted.

"All right then. I'm going to check the horses. Call if you need anything."

It was at least a quarter hour later before he heard her soft voice drifting through the trees. He gave the mare he'd been stroking a final pat, then turned and strode back to Mrs. Clark.

As she came into view around the trees, he could see she'd removed the blanket that had been covering her. The cloth now lay on the ground with the tiny baby resting atop it. Cherry wore some kind of gown and had both fists wrapped around her mother's fingers. The baby's legs kicked the air, probably enjoying the freedom of not being wrapped in all those layers.

Mrs. Clark looked up as he approached and shared that soft smile with him that she'd been giving her daughter. "I think we're feeling much better now."

He lowered himself to sit in front of a tree a couple strides away from the pair, close enough he could see the expressions on both their faces.

"She doesn't like her feet touched." Her voice kept that smile as she stroked her thumbs over the bottom of the babe's tiny feet. The infant tucked her knees, pulling away from her mother's touch, then kicked out.

He couldn't help a chuckle. "She's as ticklish as I am." He leaned closer so the baby could see his face. "I don't blame you, little girl. I don't like my feet touched either."

The baby's eyes grew round as she stared at him, her mouth puckering in a circle.

He scrambled for something else to say now that he had her attention. "You sure are a pretty thing. I never knew people could come this small. I think your feet are tinier than my thumb."

She worked her mouth like a fish as she stared at him.

So, he kept up his rambling. "How'd you like riding that horsey this morning? Did ya get a good nap? I've always thought it'd be fun to sleep on my horse. I tried it one time, but when I fell off, the ground woke me up awful quick."

Cherry shook her head, and kicked her feet out again. He'd lost her attention, but he'd held it longer than he expected.

Leaning back, he sent a grin to Mrs. Clark. "She's a cutie."

She nodded, her face softening as her focus drifted back to her daughter. Silence settled over them as she wiggled the babe's hands and stroked her legs. Her mind seemed to be somewhere else, though.

She'd probably like a moment to herself. He'd had a whole half hour to see to the horses and tend to personal things, but she'd been tied up with the baby the entire time.

He cleared the sludge from his throat. "If you'd like, I can sit with her while you take a few minutes to stretch your legs."

She jerked a look at him. Her expression seemed to be half wary, half hope. That wariness would probably win out, though. She'd already turned down one offer of help while they ate the night before.

"Are you sure you don't mind?"

Her words nearly knocked him backward. "Of course not. Miss Cherry and I'll have a nice conversation while you're gone." He smiled at the baby. "Right, little one?"

She made some kind of cooing noise as she waved her hand.

"She might get cold if I leave her on the blanket. It'd be better if you hold her." She started peeling up corners of the cloth so the baby's lower half was bundled tight. Then she scooped up the little parcel and held her out to Samuel.

He froze at the sight. He hadn't been thinking he'd hold the fragile little thing. He wanted to, but what if he accidentally hurt her? When he offered, he'd been planning just to talk and play with her. But Mrs. Clark needed a few minutes. The least he could do was hold the babe if that's what she needed.

He held out his hands the same way she had hers positioned.

She hesitated, a frown marring her brow. "Cradle your arms, and I'll set her in them."

It wasn't as easy to do that as he'd thought, but he managed to position one arm atop the other.

She eased the babe into his hold, but the bundle wasn't any heavier than the blanket alone would be.

"Are you sure she's in there? She doesn't weigh anything."

Mrs. Clark looked up at his attempt at a joke but didn't smile. "Be very careful with her head. She can't hold it up by herself, so you have to support it at all times."

"Support the head." He could barely breathe as the realization of his responsibility sank over him. This child's life was literally in his hands. He couldn't make a mistake.

Pushing down the surge of fear, he looked up to meet Mrs. Clark's gaze. "Go for a walk. We'll be right here when you get back."

She hesitated, her coffee-colored eyes troubled as they searched his. "Call me if you have trouble."

He nodded. "If I need you, I'll make sure you hear me."

She lingered another moment, then eased back, stood, and walked away.

Cherry was quiet for the first minutes. When he talked, she kept those smoky blue eyes fixed on him, so he talked until he ran out of things to say.

Then she started to fuss. She squirmed and twisted as if she was trying to wiggle out of his arms. Maybe moving a little would settle her. The rocking of the horse had sure done the trick that morning.

He eased himself to his feet—not an easy task to accomplish without jostling the wee one. The movement stopped her fidgeting, though, so he walked, shuffling around in a little circle. She seemed to like it best when he added a bounce in his step.

As he strolled around and around, bouncing and swaying, a song slipped into his mind. Maybe it was something Ma had sung. Or maybe one of his sisters. He couldn't remember all the words, but he found the tune and hummed, fitting in the words where he knew them.

As deep as it was, his voice wasn't much to listen to, but the sound seemed to fascinate little Cherry. Not only were her round eyes locked on his face, but they seemed to have a little sparkle in them.

Maybe it was ridiculous to think a baby's eyes could sparkle, but the way she looked at him tugged something deep down in his chest. He'd never imagined a little baby could affect him this much. But this little girl had lassoed him so securely, he could imagine himself giving his life to keep her safe.

The fine hairs on the back of his neck tingled, and he lifted his gaze, breaking off his song.

Mrs. Clark stood a few strides away. Motionless. Watching him.

A burn crept up his back, heating his ears. How much had she seen? Had she heard his off-key singing? He did his best to shrug his embarrassment away. "We were just taking some exercise. I think we entertained each other."

She stepped forward, and in the flickering light of the trees' shadows, it was hard to catch her expression. Softer, for sure. As she neared, her gaze locked on the child in his arms, and he couldn't help but take the opportunity to stare at Cherry's mama. She was so pretty with her tawny skin as perfect as darkened porcelain.

He shouldn't be thinking these things, but it seemed impossible not to. As long as he didn't act on his thoughts, he'd be all right.

She reached for the baby, and he held out his arms to make the child easier to grasp. Her fingers brushed his during the exchange, and the sensation that shot up his arm was like nothing he'd ever felt before. He had to work to keep from jerking back.

As Mrs. Clark snuggled the babe in her arms, Samuel couldn't help reaching out to stroke a finger over Cherry's soft hair. "Thanks for keeping me company, little one."

The babe's eyes drifted low, as though he'd completely worn her out. He knew the feeling. This last quarter hour had been more work than he'd expected, too.

Mrs. Clark raised her face to him. "Thank you. I'm ready to leave whenever you are."

Standing so near, her pretty face looking at him with that soft expression, his body had the sudden urge to step forward and kiss her.

He stepped back, forcing his mind onto her words. "I'll bring the horses around."

He needed some space to clear his head. Space...and God's help.

CHAPTER 7

"I've done everything I can, yet it seems insufficient."
~ Samuel

oriah kept one hand around the bundle strapped to her front as she eased down from her horse. Cherry had been asleep for about an hour, and she might sleep a while longer and give her mother a chance to do something helpful for once. It seemed like all day long, Mr. Grant had been doing for her, seeing to her horses, and handling her chores. The least she could do was lay out the meal for them tonight. And she was so very thirsty.

He held her mare's reins, along with those of his own horse, while she pulled out the food pack. Then she nodded her thanks, and he led the animals away. The yearling trotted along with them. The colt had done well staying with the group throughout the day, even though he ran free. It was a relief they didn't have to worry about tethering him.

Before starting on the meal, she drank her fill at the creek beside their camping spot. Nursing made her so thirsty, she'd emptied her leather canteen within an hour of leaving the creek.

The meal would be a simple affair, yet she was hungry enough to eat anything at this point. Hopefully Samuel felt the same way. She should start a fire, but every muscle in her body protested the thought of gathering wood and bending low to start the flame. Maybe they could do without.

But the night would be cold. Too cold for Cherry without a source of heat nearby. She set the food pack aside and rose to gather tender. By the time she had a flame burning, Samuel arrived with an armful of logs.

"I could've seen to the fire." He spoke in a low voice to keep from waking the baby.

She ignored the comment, both because she didn't want to chance waking Cherry and because he shouldn't have to do everything. She would handle her share of the work.

They had a nice fire leaping and had just sat down to a meal of the same cold food they'd eaten at midday when Cherry's soft grunts sounded from the blanket where she was snuggled.

Moriah put down her pemmican with a sigh. "She always seems to know when I'm about to eat."

That low, rumbling chuckle drifted from Samuel. "Shall I hold her for a minute? You must be starved."

She shook her head. "She needs to be changed and fed. I'll take my food with me while I tend her by the creek." She didn't mind him being around while the baby nursed as long as she was covered, but the process of getting to that point would require privacy.

He jumped to his feet. "Stay here and take care of her. I need to finish settling the horses anyway." He strode away before she could argue the point.

This man was so different from any she'd known before. The Indian braves kept a clear distinction between men's work and women's. And even Henry, as kind as he'd been, didn't go out of his way to help her. They'd each had their own role and had done what was expected.

But Samuel Grant... He didn't keep to the task boundaries she was accustomed to. As odd as it was, she could easily enjoy this care. Yet she couldn't allow herself to grow attached. In only a few days, he'd be on his way, and she'd never see him again.

She'd wrapped Cherry in a new cloth and nursed her, but Samuel still hadn't returned. When had she begun to think of him by his Christian name? She should call him Mr. Grant, even in her thoughts, to keep some distance.

Gathering up the baby and the bundle of soiled cloths from the day, she headed toward the creek. She'd love the chance to wash herself and rinse clean her milk-sodden shirtwaist. She did have the buckskin tunic she could change into while the fabric dried. But that might be more than her exhausted body could manage for tonight. Maybe in the morning.

Cherry played on a blanket while Moriah scrubbed the nappies in the water. The night was growing cool—cold with her hands in the icy water. She needed to get the baby bundled up, but the little one seemed to be enjoying the time to herself, cooing and babbling as she pulled a foot into her mouth.

Sounds of Samuel working drifted from the campsite as Moriah finished wringing out the last cloths. She'd have to find a way to hang them near the fire so they didn't freeze before they dried.

Was there something she should do to help Samuel before she could finally stretch out her bedroll and collapse into sleep? He'd done so much to help her these past few days, he surely expected her to handle her share of the work. More than just laying out a few bits of cold food.

Her daughter's eyes brightened when Moriah bent to bundle her in the blanket and scoop her up. Her heart lifted. No matter how weary she was, that sweet expression of love made every effort worth the cost.

Darkness was settling over the place as she stepped back into the area where the campfire blazed brightly. Samuel leaned over a bulky structure but straightened when he saw her. "I just about have this ready." He rested a hand on the top, which reached about level with his waist.

As she stepped around to see the front of it, a lump built in her throat. He'd built her a branch shelter.

"It doesn't look like rain tonight, but I thought this might give you and the baby privacy and keep you a little warmer." He shifted a branch on top.

She had to work to clear the emotion clogging her words as she raised her gaze to his. "Thank you. This will help a great deal." Being out in this open land with Cherry still so fragile had worried her more than she'd wanted to admit—even to herself. If she slept with the baby between her and the fire, what if the heat seared her little body? Or what if Moriah somehow scooted them too close to the flame? But sleeping with herself between the fire and her daughter would expose Cherry to all the cold of the night, and she had no doubt temperatures would dip below freezing before dawn came.

With this shelter, she could wrap furs around the base of the walls, creating a cocoon of warmth for the baby and keeping her far enough away from the excessive heat and dangers of the fire.

Samuel positioned more branches along the back side. "I have a couple furs you can use for bedding or to keep out the cold. I hope you have some too, 'cause mine probably won't be enough."

Those words finally broke through her haze of relief. "I do have blankets and furs in one of my packs. Are they...?"

He motioned toward a stack she'd not seen in the dim lighting. "I laid all our things there."

She moved toward the shelter. The front of it would make the perfect drying rack for the wet cloths. First, though, she had to get their bedding ready so she'd have a place to lay Cherry.

"Shall I hold her while you get things set up?" Samuel stepped around the shelter and moved near.

Cherry bounced in her arms, probably a reaction to his voice. Her daughter had connected with him so easily, Moriah might be jealous if it wasn't so sweet.

She turned to gauge whether Samuel really meant his offer. Hadn't he had enough of them and their neediness for one day?

But his gaze had found her daughter where she lay against Moriah's shoulder. And the soft expression on his face took away her hesitation. "Thank you."

She raised the babe and lay her in the cradle he formed with his arms. His skin was warm as her fingers brushed his palm, and part of her wanted to jerk away. He didn't flinch though, and that gave her strength to hold her ground.

"Hey there, pumpkin." He spoke in that deep, gentle timbre as he held her daughter close, bouncing a little.

She stepped back, taking in the picture they made. The great, strong man holding close the tiny bundle of innocence. Emotion rose up to clog her throat again. She could watch this pair for hours.

But instead, she forced herself to turn away and do the work that stretched before her.

~

Samuel used a fork to flip a johnnycake in the pan the next morning. The smell of it called to him, even though this food surely wouldn't be as tasty as the pemmican Mrs. Clark had served the day before. That stuff seemed to be an entire meal cooked inside little flat cakes, including berries, meat, and who knew what else.

But warm food—even simple johnnycakes—would do them both good. He'd heard the babe awaken several times through the night, and the sounds of stirring lasted for a good half hour each time. No wonder Mrs. Clark kept those dark valleys under eyes. He would let her sleep as long as she could, then have a warm meal ready when she awoke.

He didn't have long to wait. The sound of a tiny yawn drifted from the shelter, and he couldn't help a glance. The blankets were wiggling, and a little fist poked out. Maybe he should try to pull Cherry away so her mother could sleep a bit longer.

But as he neared, the blankets shifted more, easing down to reveal glossy brown hair. Mrs. Clark's pretty features were softened in the morning light.

He stilled, not quite able to take his eyes off of her. She must have sensed his presence, for she turned, her brown eyes taking him in. For a long moment, their gazes held, and he wasn't sure what passed between them. Maybe simply an awareness. But he couldn't bring himself to look away, not until she broke the hold as she turned to look at her daughter.

Easing back, he inhaled a lungful of chilly air. He had to get a grip on himself before he did something that would break her trust.

After filling a plate with the flapjacks and a cup with water he'd kept simmering, he turned back to Mrs. Clark. "I've some warm food and water here for you. Just let me know when you're ready for it." He couldn't tell what she was doing in there, fussing with blankets or something, her back turned to him. He tried not to look, just in case.

She glanced over her shoulder. "Thank you. If you'll set it down beside me, that would be wonderful."

He did as she said, placing the dishes just at the edge of the shelter. "I'm gonna check on the horses. Call out if you need anything."

Her attention was still occupied inside the shelter, so he stepped back, then turned and walked away. The animals had to be his focus now.

And a welcome change. Horses he knew. Women and babies were foreign territory.

~

Samuel glanced over his shoulder to look for the yearling later that morning. The horse had been growing braver as they rode, lingering back until he was almost out of sight before tearing forward to catch up. Now midway through the afternoon, the colt was still up to the same tricks.

"Is he coming?" Mrs. Clark rode beside him, little Cherry awake for once in the sling hanging from her neck.

"I think I still see him, but he's not coming yet." He really didn't want to have to put the colt on a lead line. The horse seemed barely halter broken, and it would likely be a fight to keep him moving with them, even though his mother was the pack horse tethered to Samuel's gelding.

Just then, that same mare raised her head and nickered.

"Thatta girl." Samuel reached back to scratch the mare's forelock. "Call your boy."

A squeal sounded in the distance behind them. Then a speck of brown came tearing toward them, bucking as he ran. The colt loosed another cry as he paused to rear up, his front legs striking the air wildly.

"What in the world?" Samuel tightened his grip on his reins so his own gelding didn't get nervous from the shenanigans.

The horse tore forward again, galloping full-tilt toward them like fire was licking his hooves. When he reached them, he didn't stop, but veered around in a high-speed circle.

"I think there's something on his muzzle."

Samuel saw the shadow just as Mrs. Clark spoke. Like oversize whiskers poking out from the tender flesh of his nose.

A knot tightened in Samuel's gut. *Porcupine quills.*

This wouldn't be easy. He slid off his horse and looked around for a place to tie the animal. No trees for quite a distance. And he couldn't leave his gelding ground tied because of the mare tethered behind the saddle. Too much chance for something to go wrong.

"I'll hold him." Mrs. Clark reached for the reins. She already had little Cherry to worry about, but he didn't have another choice. He had to get those quills out of the colt's skin before he really hurt himself.

CHAPTER 8

"The farther we travel, the more thankful I am that I don't travel alone."
~ Moriah

*S*amuel handed over the reins, then untied the rope hanging from the pack mare's saddle. The colt had slowed his frantic circling and now charged toward Samuel where he stood beside the mare.

"Easy, boy." He tried to catch the yearling's neck, but the animal barged through his grip and pressed against the mare—his mother.

She squealed and kicked out when the porcupine barbs pressed against the soft flesh of her flank, and the colt jerked back as though he'd touched a hot anvil. The contact must've pushed the quills farther into his own skin.

Samuel sidestepped to get out of the mare's kicking range, then turned his focus to the yearling. "Come on, boy. Let me help you." He eased toward where the colt stood heaving, hooves spread and mouth open, as though trying to take in air that way instead of through his pain-riddled nose. His tongue hung to the side.

Poor horse. A pinch of fear slipped through Samuel's chest. Could the colt die from this episode? As long as Samuel could get the quills out, he was pretty sure the animal would be fine. But what if the young thing's heart couldn't bear the strain? If he didn't settle down, his condition could get a lot worse. And the last thing Mrs. Clark needed was to lose one of her horses, too.

Keeping one hand outstretched, he eased the rope into position with his other so he could send the loop over the horse's head. He was close now, within five strides. The yearling made a hoarse choking sound in his throat, then turned and bolted, flinging his head with every few strides.

Determination slipped into place inside Samuel. It was time to step up his efforts. While the colt ran in a wide circle around them, bucking and trying to escape the pain from the porcupine quills, Samuel worked a loop into his rope like he'd used when catching calves for branding back on the Van Vleck ranch in California.

After he had the rope ready, it took a couple more minutes for the colt to slow and draw near enough. Samuel swung the loop in a steady circle around his own head, gaining momentum to toss it over the horse.

Those years of working on the ranch paid off. Samuel slid the rope over the animal's head with the first throw. The loop must have brushed the spikes as it landed, for the colt jerked back, bobbing his head wildly. When he felt the tension of the loop around his neck, he exploded, jerking hard against the rope. Scrambling, almost sitting down on his haunches.

Samuel fought to hold the rope, easing forward to loosen the loop and give the animal enough slack to breathe. He couldn't let the horse get away. The sting of the fibers bit into his palms, making him long for a pair of gloves.

As the colt struggled to keep his footing, all the while fighting to get away from this new terror, Samuel moved forward to loosen the rope. He was probably going to have to tie the colt down to remove the barbs, something he wasn't looking forward to.

This poor animal was out of its mind with fear and pain. The sooner they got this done, the better.

By the time he finally had the yearling down, lying on the ground with three legs tied, Samuel and the animal were a sweaty, exhausted mess. The horse's sides heaved, and more whites showed in his fearful eyes than the normal dark coloring.

Samuel eased down next to the colt's head, then stroked his forelock and the blaze splashed across his face. "It's all right, boy. We're gonna get you taken care of. Hang in there for me."

There had to be at least twenty quills stuck in the tender flesh of the horse's muzzle, most poking an inch or so out. Samuel reached for one of the closest. The moment he touched it, the horse jerked back, bobbing his nose and opening his mouth wide again, tongue hanging to the side like before. Such a pitiful sight.

"Easy, boy." He went back to stroking so the animal would settle, then looked up and scanned the area.

Mrs. Clark stood a dozen strides away, holding the other three horses, Cherry tucked in the sling in front of her. Concern marred the woman's face. "What can I do?"

There was no way he was letting her or that fragile baby near this crazed animal. And he couldn't think of anything in his packs that would help with the job ahead. A good pair of forceps would be the thing, but he didn't have a set with him. Hadn't expected to need them.

He shook his head. "Just keep yourself and the baby safe. And if you can keep those horses quiet, that'd be helpful too. If they put you in danger though, let them go."

Turning his focus back to the colt, he analyzed the locations of each barb. Most of them were on the front and left side of the face, so it might be best if he jerked the two needles on the right side out quickly, then tried to keep the horse's head lying flat on that side.

Thankfully, both of those quills were thick enough he could get a decent grip on them. The horse jerked when he felt the touch, but Samuel was prepared for the response and used the colt's efforts to help extract the needle.

He eased out a breath as he held the skinny thing between his fingers. Amazing how a little barb like this could send a mighty horse into a tumble. It took several moments of soothing and stroking before the colt stilled enough for him to pull out the second quill on that side.

Again, the horse jerked and bobbed its head, but some of the strength seemed to be easing out of its protests.

"Thatta, boy." Samuel stroked his forehead again, then eased around and gently lowered his knee to rest on the horse's neck. Hopefully, this would help the colt feel a little more secure and make him stop fighting. It sure helped with the calves during branding.

By the time he'd pulled half a dozen more quills, the colt had stopped fighting. Samuel kept up a steady crooning and did his best not to let his own nerves bunch up as he pulled spike after spike from the colt's nose. Blood seeped from the empty holes, and it didn't take long before they were both smeared in crimson.

At last, he pulled the final quill from the colt's lower lip. He rubbed his hand once more over every part of horse's muzzle to check for any he'd missed, smearing more blood in the process. His skin felt only whiskers, not the stiff fibers of the porcupine quills.

"We're done." He eased his knee off the colt's neck, then stroked that part of him. "I hope you learned your lesson. I sure don't want either of us to go through this again."

With a final gentle pat, he pulled the rope off the horse's neck, then moved down to untie his legs. When he was free, the colt didn't seem to want to move. Samuel stood and shifted around to stand behind him, giving him an upward push.

That set the horse in motion, and he scrambled to his feet, then stood with feet spread, gulping in big breaths. Samuel stepped close again and stroked the horse's neck. "I need to spend more time with you, I think. I'm sure Mrs. Clark hasn't been able to, but you need more experience around people. It'd do you good."

At last, he turned his weary body back to where Mrs. Clark still stood with the horses. The toll of the ordeal seemed to have settled into every one of his muscles and bones. He'd not felt this worn-out since his days on the ranch.

He strode forward, stumbling a little over his own feet as he walked. He had to pull himself together. The day wasn't anywhere near over.

As he drew near, Mrs. Clark studied his face, her gaze taking in everything. He reached for his reins, and she allowed him to pull them from her grasp. Yet her brows furrowed as she watched him.

"I think we should stop for the night." She reached up and touched his temple, wiping what must be a smear of blood. Her touch seared his skin, sending a tingle all the way down his back. It wasn't a hurried touch, yet she didn't linger overlong either.

Her gaze dropped from his face, drifting off into the distance. "As soon as we find water, we make camp."

His body was still reeling so much from the impact of her fingers on his skin, he couldn't have denied her if he'd wanted to. And her idea sounded perfect to him.

"All right. Are you and Little Bit unhurt?" He looked down at the babe, who lay snuggled against her mother, one tiny fist up next to her face. So peaceful.

"We're well. Ours was the easy task."

He looked up at her and tried to summon a smile. "I hope he learned his lesson about porcupines."

Her smile was soft, so beautiful it made his chest ache.

With all the willpower he had left, he turned and positioned the horses so Mrs. Clark and he could mount up. Even if they camped soon, he and this woman still had a long evening ahead.

~

*W*hile Mrs. Clark nursed the babe, Samuel took a few minutes for a much-needed bath. Not a full dunking, but he stripped his bloody shirt off and washed from the waist up, then scrubbed out the sweat and dirt and everything else clogging the fabric. Good thing he'd brought an extra shirt, 'cause there was no way he could have stood himself in this one for another day.

When he was done, he checked the horses once more before gathering an armload of wood. The colt was stretched out in the grass near his mother, worn out from the day's ordeal. His face was probably still sensitive. Samuel would need to keep an eye on him to make sure he ate enough while the wounds healed.

As he neared the place where he'd left woman and child, he made his steps a little heavier so she would hear him coming. When only a thin layer of trees stood between him and the camp, he stopped. "Is it all right if I come closer?"

"Come." Mrs. Clark's voice was always soft, but he could hear the added weariness in just that word.

He stepped between the last of the trees, his gaze taking in the woman leaning over the makings of a fire. Little Cherry lay on a blanket behind her mother, gurgling and cooing.

He eased his load of wood beside a tree where it would be out of the way. "I can take care of that." He motioned toward the tiny flame she'd sheltered inside a tent of birch bark.

She straightened, and the weary curve of her shoulders was hard to miss.

He dropped to his knees beside her where he could continue to nurture the fire. "Why don't you go refresh yourself at the creek? Cherry and I will have the fire built up by the time you get back." He offered what he hoped was a competent grin, but his tired muscles had trouble holding the expression.

Her gaze searched his face. "Are you sure?"

He gripped her upper arm. "I'm sure. Take a few minutes, you've earned them." In the seconds their gazes held, the realization of what he'd done sank through him.

He'd touched her. Was still touching her. He dropped his hand to his lap as heat flamed up his neck. Turning to the fire, he leaned forward and tucked a few fragments of bark into the flame.

She didn't move at first, still kneeling beside him. He'd positioned himself too close to her. Maybe that was his first mistake. But he'd expected her to rise, leaving him in the right place to tend the fire.

Finally, she stood. "You're sure you don't mind watching her?"

He straightened, brushing bark from his hands. "I'd like to see her for a bit. We haven't had much chance to visit today, have we, Miss Cherry?" He shifted closer to the little one and peered down at her.

After another moment, Mrs. Clark padded away, taking the weight of her presence with her.

He did get the fire burning, but he had to admit he spent most of the time Mrs. Clark was gone playing with the baby. That little thing didn't have many expressions yet, but she still found a way to get her point across. She was certainly ticklish on her tiny feet, and he was pretty sure she gave a real smile at one point.

Mrs. Clark's quiet steps slipped into his awareness, and he raised his gaze to her. In truth, she was like true north to his compass, drawing his focus no matter where she was. But this time as he looked, his breath caught in his throat. Her dark brown hair was damp and slicked back, taking on the shimmer of a crow's wing. The weary lines around her eyes had disappeared, making her look so fresh and beautiful, his chest squeezed tight.

And the softness in her eyes as she met his gaze was almost his undoing. He sat back on his heels, scrambling for something to say. Trying to patch the fragments of his scattered thoughts back together. "I, um, can get started heating food. The fire's hot now."

She moved toward the pack where they'd combined their food supplies. "I'll make stew and you sit. But don't think you have to entertain the babe. She's content on her own."

Sitting here watching Mrs. Clark prepare the meal sounded just shy of heavenly. And not just because every part of his body ached. Watching this woman was like watching a deer run, all grace and agile movements. And every part of her beautiful.

He stretched out next to Cherry and let her grasp the strands of his hair and tug, something she'd already shown she liked to do. Sometimes she'd get his nose instead, and he pretended to eat her hand. She hadn't yet learned to laugh, of course, but he could almost hear the giggle in the light of her eyes.

Playing with her seemed to awaken something inside him he hadn't known he possessed. Something warm and protective that made his chest ache. If he had to put a name to it, he might call it love. This wasn't his baby—not by a long shot—but with every passing hour, he could imagine less and less how his life would continue without her.

CHAPTER 9

"I've learned to trust the senses God gave me."
~ Samuel

$\mathcal{B}$y the time Mrs. Clark had the stew tucked in beside the fire to cook, Samuel knew he had to get up and set to work. He'd dawdled too long, although he wouldn't have traded a minute of his time with the little angel, watching her mother prepare the food.

"All right, pumpkin. It's time I get started on your house for tonight." He pushed up to sitting and gave her tiny foot a last tap.

Mrs. Clark turned to him as he rose. "Thank you for playing with her. She really enjoys it." Again, that smile. Something about her seemed so much softer this evening, emphasizing her beauty. He'd been aware of how pretty she was from their first meeting, but it hadn't reached out and clutched hold of him every time he looked at her—not like it did tonight.

"I had more fun than she did, no doubt." He tried to keep his words light. Tried not to betray the depth of the thoughts and feelings rooting deeper inside him.

It was high time he focus on his work. "Is there anything you need before I get started on the shelter?"

Her eyes widened the tiniest bit. "Thank you, no. The meal should be ready when you're done."

The thought of food brought to life the empty places in his belly. "Sounds good. I'll work fast." He reached out and touched her arm as he stepped by her. And it wasn't until he'd passed her and started into the woods that he realized what he'd done.

Touched her again. Why was he doing that? He certainly wasn't a fellow who went around laying hands on people. Yet twice this evening, he'd reached out and made contact with her before he realized what he'd done.

He was losing his mind. If he'd focus more on his work and less on the females in his party, maybe he'd stop doing irrational things.

The area around their camp didn't have many low-hanging branches, so he had to travel down the creek before he found enough to build the shelter. As he collected the last of the boughs for the frame, his neck tingled with awareness. Was someone watching him?

Keeping his manner easy, he slid his glance back toward the camp. He could see the horses grazing just outside the woods, but trees blocked his view of Mrs. Clark and their campfire. Had she followed him? Come to ask something?

Yet he didn't see her figure anywhere among the trunks around him. He did his best to keep from showing his tension as he made the final cut in the tree branch. When he stooped to pick-up the armful of logs and branches, he used the opportunity to scan the rest of the woods behind him.

No shifting shadows. Nothing that looked out of place. Maybe the unease was all in his mind. The Lord knew his head was certainly off-kilter tonight.

But he'd keep his guard up anyway. If someone was lurking around, watching them, the reason couldn't be good. A friendly man would show himself.

It looked like the night would be a long one, but he'd do what was necessary to keep them safe. He'd been granted precious goods to protect, and there was no way he'd let anything happen to either of them.

~

The cold dug deep into Moriah's bones through the night, more frigid than any night on their journey so far. She had to fight hard to keep Cherry warm enough. Samuel stirred more than usual, too, and he kept the fire blazing strong. There simply wasn't much they could do to ward off the force of winter as they neared the mountains.

They set out early the next morning, since moving seemed the only thing to ward off the chill. She kept Cherry wrapped in a fur inside the sling, and pulled a second fur around them both.

The landscape was gradually shifting into the hilly terrain that came just before the mountains. She still remembered the day three years before when she'd traveled this same path with Henry—going the opposite direction.

She'd been so afraid, yet she'd done her best not to let her fear show. Grandfather trusted Henry Clark, so she'd told herself she should too. But she'd been raised with stories of the brutality of her own father and his cohorts, which pounded the fear of white men deep inside her.

She'd not been willing to admit it at the time, but now she could see the root of bitterness that had grown in her toward her grandfather. If he loved her as much as she'd always thought, he wouldn't have given her to a white man. At least, that had been her thought in those awful days.

But her grandfather had been right about Henry. As hard as it had been to leave her people and enter the strange life at the fort, he'd been good to her. Kind and patient. When she couldn't stand another day among those men, he'd built her a house two hours' ride away from them. A beautiful cabin—the nicest home she'd ever had.

And now she'd walked away from that home as though it were nothing. As though Henry and the life he'd worked so hard to build for them were meaningless.

She had to move forward. Had to find a place suitable for Cherry to grow up. The safety of the life she'd been raised in would be perfect. She couldn't help craving that life, even now. Sure, living among people had its dangers. But those were dangers she knew well.

Samuel eased his horse back to ride alongside her. "How are you both holding up?" There came his easy grin, the one that always soothed her insides. Except this time the smile didn't quite reach his eyes. Maybe the cold was taking a toll on him, too.

She pulled the fur tighter around herself and the baby. "We're well. Probably warmer than you are." She nodded toward his buckskin jacket. It was sturdy enough, but he'd need a buffalo coat if he planned to last the winter in the mountains.

He tucked his chin into his collar as if she'd reminded him of how cold he was. "We can stop for the midday meal at those trees up ahead. Maybe build a fire and heat the rest of that good stew you made last night. That should help warm us from the inside."

A wonderful idea, although it would slow down their travels. Good thing they'd started early that morning.

When they reached the thin row of trees bordering a narrow stream, Samuel helped her dismount and took her reins. "You take care of yourself and the baby. I'll get a fire going." He sent a glance around the area, then back over his shoulder the way they'd come.

"Thank you." She shouldn't let him take over all the work. But Cherry was starting to fuss, probably both hungry and cold from her soiled cloth. Moriah draped the fur over herself and the babe to keep them warm as she worked quickly to change her.

She'd become adept at getting the nursing process started quickly, so by the time Samuel returned to build the fire, she was settled with the furs wrapped around her.

An icy breeze blew out his flame twice before he was able to shield the area enough for the blaze to take hold. As he waited, protecting the tiny fire with his body, his focus shifted to scan their surroundings. He seemed to have done that a lot since they'd stopped.

"Are you looking for something?"

His gaze jerked to her. "I keep getting the feeling someone's watching. I haven't seen anyone, but I can't shake it."

She straightened. She'd been so focused on Cherry and keeping them both warm, she'd let her other senses slip. Grandfather would be disappointed.

Letting herself feel her surroundings, she pulled the fur tighter around herself and the nursing babe. "How long have you sensed this person?"

"Since last eve. Like I said, I haven't *seen* even a hint of anyone. It's just a gut feeling. Maybe only my imagination."

She knew better than to think that. She leveled her gaze on Samuel. "We need to trap him. Make him think we're leaving, then circle back."

He nodded grimly, his look making it clear he didn't think the feeling was only his imagination. "I was thinking when we leave these trees, maybe I could tether my horses to yours and let you ride on. I'll hide here and wait 'til he shows himself."

She fought the urge to draw her knees up into herself. She felt safe with Samuel, but if there was another white man lurking out there, who knew what evil he intended. She forced herself to nod. "I can do that." She had her gun and knife. If the man overcame Samuel and came after her, she'd do what she had to for protection.

That thought pressed hard on her chest. She didn't want anything to happen to Samuel. He'd been so good to her, how could she leave him to fend for himself? But he was strong. Capable. He'd have the upper hand on whatever adversary skulked out there.

Still, she turned and found his gaze with her own. "Be careful. Please."

He held her look as he nodded. "I will. Just look natural as you ride away, and I'll take care of things here." Then a line creased his brow. "Will it be too much to manage? The horses and Little Bit there?" He nodded toward Cherry.

She shook her head. "I can do it." That was the least of her worries. With Cherry in a sling and the horses tethered appropriately, she'd be fine. The yearling had been staying close since his ordeal with the porcupine, so that made the job even easier.

Within a half hour, they were both sitting close to the fire, sipping warm stew, yet all the joy she'd anticipated from the meal was gone. Stolen away as she listened for any snap of a twig or rustle of a leaf.

"Is Little Bit staying warm enough?" Samuel nodded toward the baby cradled in her lap.

"I think so. I have her wrapped up so tightly, the cold can't get through." She adjusted the fur covering.

"Did you have any brothers or sisters?"

She jerked her gaze up to his face. He'd not asked such a personal question before. His head was cocked in relaxed curiosity.

He must have sensed her hesitation, for he spoke again. "I just mean to say, you're a really good mother. It makes me think you had siblings you helped raise. My sister Noelle is like that. She half-raised my brothers and me, and she's right at home with her own young'uns."

His sister. She'd like to hear more about his family, but she owed him an answer to his question first.

"I have two half-brothers older, and two half-sisters younger." Perhaps she shouldn't have given so much detail, but she'd never been able to hide her past. The entire camp had known of the horrors of her conception.

If he was surprised by what she said, he didn't show it. "Right in the middle, huh? Just like Noelle. I'm sure you were a lot of help with the little ones."

She'd tried to be. It seemed like she'd always been trying to make up for her birth, the unspeakable things her father had done to her mother.

She forced the memories aside and turned her focus on him. "So, you have a brother and a sister?"

His mouth tugged into a wry grin. "Four brothers and four sisters.

Seth, the one who's marrying your sister-in-law, is my twin. There's one brother younger than us, but all the rest are older."

It took a moment for his words to sort themselves in her mind. "Nine of you?" His poor mother. "How many of you share the same father?"

His brows rose the tiniest bit. "All of us. Same saintly mother and same hardworking father." He paused a moment, then his voice softened. "I didn't appreciate them the way I should have before I left home. They're good people."

A wave of longing slipped through her. To have both parents throughout his life? She couldn't imagine how wonderful that must be. Her mother had been the one constant in her life. Red Hawk, who'd fathered the rest of her siblings, had died before the youngest was even born, so she had only a few memories of him.

Of course, Grandfather had always been there. Grave and solid. And she'd never doubted his love for her. Not until he married her to Henry anyway, but even that had been better than she'd thought it would be.

Samuel breathed out a long sigh as he lowered his bowl to his lap. "That was even better today than last night. I must say, you're an excellent cook, Mrs. Clark."

Heat slid up her neck, warming her all the way through. She dipped her chin. "I'm glad you liked it." Was she so starved for appreciation she now blushed like a maiden?

Yet kind words from this man felt different from others she'd received. The way he looked at her, the gentle way he spoke—they did funny things in her middle. A feeling she'd do best to ignore.

She straightened. "I guess it's time to clean up, then put our plan into action."

He nodded. "Guess so." But he was slow to move. And a small part of her wondered if he hesitated because he enjoyed her company.

But that was a silly thought. One that would only bring her trouble.

CHAPTER 10

"One more thing I did not expect."
~ Moriah

Samuel's gut clenched tightly as he watched Mrs. Clark ride away, the three horses trailing her mount. Was he sending her into danger?

He had no idea what he'd find as he waited here. He only knew he had to find out what trouble had been lurking about, watching them. The farther they traveled today, the more certain his instincts had become. And twice, he'd thought he'd seen the outline of a dark head rise above the line of grass behind them, then duck down again. Someone was purposely staying just out of sight to avoid discovery. He couldn't imagine why a man would go through that much effort, unless his plans were sinister.

Lord, don't let him realize Mrs. Clark is riding away alone. He was counting on the trees to shield her from clear view.

Forcing his gaze away from the solitary form of the woman, he scanned the landscape behind them. He'd positioned himself in the fork of a tree trunk, about a stride up from the ground, where he'd have enough height to see the stranger clearly. There were enough leafless branches that he and his rifle would blend into the landscape, as long as he didn't move. Even then, a man wouldn't be able to make him out from a distance.

Within ten minutes, Samuel's foot had gone to sleep where it pressed into the narrow joint of the trunk. He'd been much more agile at climbing trees when he was a boy. He shifted his footing, trying to work out a better position.

Then a movement in the distance caught his eye. A brown dot on the horizon, bouncing and growing as it moved closer.

A man on horseback? No, as the full body crested the hill, he could see it was only a man. Running.

He kept up a steady jog, coming over the path they'd traveled less than an hour ago. His buckskins almost blended with the brown winter grass, and the stranger moved lithely, as though he could keep up that run for miles.

Who was he? And why on foot? They were days away from Fort Hamilton, but it was possible he lived somewhere in this area. Had he been following them since the night before? And why?

Minutes passed as the man neared, keeping up that steady jog.

Samuel tightened his grip on his rifle as the imposter reached the trees in the exact place they'd built their warming fire. He paused, propping his hands at his waist as his shoulders rose and fell with his deep breathing. Then he stared off into the distance, and Samuel followed his gaze.

Mrs. Clark and the horses were still in sight, mounting a gentle hill that would soon shelter them from this man's sight. It was plain to see only one person was riding away. Samuel's gut tightened as he shifted his focus back to the stranger.

The man was gone.

Samuel tightened his grip on his rifle and positioned it to fire, should he need to. The fellow must have slipped behind a tree. Maybe he'd noticed only one figure rode atop the distant horses.

He strained to see between the shifting branches, searching for the light brown of the man's buckskins.

There. Wasn't that him? The sliver of brown beside the tree disappeared, but that must have been his arm.

Samuel had to take control of the situation before he lost the stalker. He was in a vulnerable position up in the tree, though. He needed to get to the ground without the man pulling a gun on him. Why had he thought this was a good position?

Easing down, he worked to stay completely soundless. The fellow must have seen him to know how to remain hidden behind the tree, but Samuel still didn't want to give away his movements.

When he had both feet on the ground, he aimed his rifle squarely at the tree where the man was hiding. "I have a rifle aimed at you. Come out from behind that tree and keep your hands where I can see them."

Silence fell over the area. A deep quiet that tightened the knot in his gut. Would the stranger obey or try to make a run for it? If he ran, Samuel would have to stop him. The obvious threat couldn't be left to haunt them. He would aim for a leg or something that wouldn't be life-threatening, but would stop the fellow.

He deepened his voice to a menacing tone. "This is your last chance to step out peacefully before I start shooting."

Let him step out, Lord. His stomach churned as he aimed down the barrel.

A flash of brown appeared at the edge of the tree. Samuel tensed. Not a flash, a slow, solid movement.

The arm shifted to reveal the rest of the body, and the man stepped fully into view. Samuel tensed, keeping his aim as he took in the stranger.

Dark features, lean body. Very lean. He was clad in buckskins with a rifle slung over his shoulder, held by a leather strap. Samuel's gaze narrowed on his face.

He wasn't much more than a boy.

"Who are you?" Samuel barked.

The man-boy eyed him warily, a shock of black hair shadowing his eyes. His skin wasn't dark enough to be full Indian, but he certainly looked like he might have some of that blood running through him.

Like Mrs. Clark. The thought jolted through him. Was this boy related to her? Was that why he'd been following?

"Who are you?" He softened his tone just a little, keeping enough steel to hopefully stop the lad from attempting to run. He wasn't sure he could bring himself to shoot a boy who looked to be just old enough for his voice to have deepened.

He couldn't let him get away without answers, though. And did he even understand English? If he'd been raised with the natives, maybe not.

The lad raised his chin. "I am Matisse."

A bit of the tension eased from Samuel's chest. The lad understood and wasn't refusing to speak. "And why have you been following us, Matisse?"

The boy eyed him, not giving a hint of what he might be thinking behind that dark gaze. Then finally, he spoke again. "I don't follow. I go to the same place as you."

His words had a slight accent. Just barely there. Almost like the lilting flow of Mrs. Clark's speech. Was he part of the same band of Peigan? "Where is it you're going exactly?"

"To my people."

"Which people?"

The boy raised his chin again. "Those who gave me life."

This was getting them nowhere. Samuel leveled him with a gaze that he hoped would make the boy squirm until the truth slipped out. "You say you weren't following, but I've felt your presence with us for a while now, yet you never showed yourself. Why did you hide?"

The boy eyed him with a glare, not saying a word.

Samuel allowed the silence to stretch out. Let the lad feel the weight of it so maybe he'd break down and answer.

What were they going to do with him? Samuel was no longer as worried about the danger this scrawny overgrown lad would provide, but he'd feel much better if he could keep an eye on Matisse instead of turning him loose to follow and snoop again.

Should he trust the boy around Mrs. Clark and the baby? If Samuel allowed a danger into their camp and either of them came to harm, he'd never forgive himself.

Still, maybe she knew this boy. If they were from the same band, there was a good chance she did. And if not, he'd like to know her thoughts on what to do with him.

He motioned with his rifle. "It's time we catch up with my group. Start walking."

The boy eyed him a final time, then obeyed. Turning toward the path Mrs. Clark had taken, he marched forward. *Thank you, Lord.*

Samuel followed a few strides behind him, his gun still aimed at the lad. He wasn't sure he could shoot the boy even if he ran, but hopefully keeping the rifle aimed would dissuade him from attempting anything ill-advised.

As they trekked toward the distant rise, it soon became clear Matisse was much better at hiking through the wilderness than Samuel was. He tried to keep his breathing steady so he didn't give away the effort their clip took to maintain. Matisse didn't seem winded at all, just settled into his lanky stride.

At last they crested the knoll Mrs. Clark had ridden over, and Samuel eased out a breath of relief. There she sat, still astride her mare with the other horses tethered behind her. The sling with Cherry inside was draped across her front as usual.

Her gaze met his first, and something like relief eased her features. Then her focus shifted to the lad, eyes narrowing, as though she wasn't quite sure what she was seeing.

He knew the feeling.

When they were a half dozen strides away, he barked, "That's far enough."

Matisse stopped. Samuel couldn't see his expression, since he was behind the boy, but he could tell he was eyeing Mrs. Clark.

And she him, except a softness had taken over her features. A gentleness, almost motherly. Her gaze lifted to Samuel in question.

He motioned toward the lad. "This is Matisse. He says he's not following us, only going the same direction we are. To his people. That's all he's said so far."

She shifted her focus back to the boy and spoke, yet the words flowed in a language he couldn't understand. Peigan?

Samuel eased around so he could see the boy's face. Confusion. And maybe a little disappointment.

Then the lad raised his chin and spoke in English. "I am Peigan, but I don't know the tongue. I was raised by a white man, a trapper who is no longer of this world. I now go back to those who gave me life."

"Whose people are you from? Who is the leader?" Mrs. Clark seemed to be attempting to keep her emotions from showing on her face, but her eyes sparkled with a hint of the excitement she must surely be feeling. This boy could be kin to her.

Matisse's face took on a bit of uncertainty. "I'm not certain. Pierre found me by a hot spring, about a half days' ride in to the mountains. It was winter, and he said the Indians had already left the area. He took me to his cabin but never found the people I came from."

A line formed across her forehead. "How old were you? Is Matisse your Indian name or did Pierre give it to you?"

"He thinks I was two when he found me, and he named me."

The lad was certainly answering her questions better than he had Samuel's. But he couldn't blame the boy. With her pretty eyes seeking him out, she would be impossible to resist.

And it probably helped that she wasn't pointing a gun at him.

There was one thing that still bothered Samuel, though. He'd feel better if he asked it now instead of after the boy joined their group, as he suspected would be the case. "How is it you found us? And how did you know we're going to a Piegan camp?"

The lad swiveled to face him, his expression turning more guarded. But he still answered. "I saw men on the trail. Heard them talk about meeting a man and woman going into the mountains to find her Indian people. I thought following you would be my best chance."

So, he had been following. But Samuel wouldn't call him on the lie he'd told earlier. This boy was simply desperate and finding his way the best he could. He probably didn't know who to trust. "How old are you, son?" He shifted around to get a better view of the boy's responses.

Matisse raised his chin. "Fifteen. I think."

Samuel nodded. A year or so older than he'd have guessed, but still too young to be on his own in this wilderness. Especially with winter coming on.

He turned to Mrs. Clark, studying her face for any sign of lingering fear toward the lad. Inviting him into their camp would require a measure of trust.

She returned Samuel's gaze, eyes glistening. Then she gave an almost imperceptible nod of agreement. Good.

He looked at Matisse. "If you'd like to join in with us, you can. We're going to Mrs. Clark's people, a Peigan camp about a day's ride into the mountains. We'd expect you to help with what needs done, and you're welcome to share our food."

The boy's gaze turned wary, and he gazed from Samuel to Mrs. Clark. His eyes looked to be almost asking her for permission.

She nodded. "We'd like you to join us. It would help us all." Based on her tone, she seemed to be trying to maintain her distance, but it wasn't hard to feel her warmth.

Matisse turned back to Samuel with a nod. "I will do my part."

"All right then." He let out a breath as he turned his focus to what should be done next. They needed to get on the trail, but the boy certainly couldn't walk. He looked to Mrs. Clark. "I think we could move the packs around to let him ride the other mare."

She nodded. "I can carry more behind my saddle."

Within a few minutes Samuel had the gear shifted to allow Matisse to ride. Samuel hesitated a long moment over the rifle slung behind the boy's back. It seemed like a bad idea to take the weapon away, an act that would only build distrust and bitterness in the lad. They just had a couple of days to travel, but the coming terrain would require them to work together, each looking out for the good of the group.

So he didn't speak of the gun, just held the horse while the boy mounted. "You've ridden before?"

Matisse nodded and took up the reins. He seemed to know what he was doing, although he was a bit stiff in the saddle. He would grow more comfortable in time.

Samuel turned back to untether his gelding from Mrs. Clark's mare but paused at her side, raising his hand to shield his eyes from the midday sun as he studied her. "How's Little Bit doing?" He tapped one end of the bundle of furs. They were tucked so tightly, from this angle, he couldn't tell where the babe was among the pelts. "Is she staying warm enough?"

Mrs. Clark looked down. "I think so. She's sleeping now." Then she raised her gaze to his, and the power of her beautiful eyes speared all the way to his core. It took everything in him not to reach up and touch her. Not to take her hand.

Did she think of him as more than someone to help on the journey? He wanted to be a help to her, but with each passing hour, he wanted to be more.

Yet she was mourning her dead husband. His thoughts were way out of line.

Forcing himself to step away, he turned toward his gelding. His only focus should be to get this woman and her baby to her family safely. And he should add getting Matisse there, as well.

He mounted his horse and squared his shoulders. Time to accomplish the mission God had assigned him and stop wishing for what would never happen.

CHAPTER 11

"God, this I'm not prepared for. Show me what to do."
~ Samuel

*M*oriah couldn't help but find it amusing to watch Samuel with Matisse that evening. He studied the boy's every movement like a hawk scrutinizing prey.

If there was one thing she'd learned about Samuel Grant, it was his kindness, so she wasn't worried overmuch about the boy. Once he proved trustworthy, Samuel would ease his watchfulness.

In truth, she should probably be more concerned about having a stranger travel with them. But something about this boy rang true in her spirit. It wasn't just his youthfulness—she'd seen plenty of young men whom she wouldn't trust farther than the end of her arm. But the earnestness in his eyes—and something in his manner—eased her guard aside.

Samuel, on the other hand, seemed to take more convincing. Seeing his protectiveness wrapped a warm feeling around her like thick fur to block out the buffeting wind. Throughout the evening, he never left her sight unless Matisse was with him.

And with two pairs of hands to help with the camp, she didn't feel as pressured to carry an equal part of the load. Not that she'd managed anywhere near that much yet, with all the tending Cherry required.

Night hung around them as the little group sat by the campfire, eating from a pot of beans. The warm food helped offset the frigid air blowing off the mountains. She'd not had a chance to talk with Matisse, as Samuel had kept him working, gathering wood for the fire and branches for her shelter.

Now, she focused her attention on the lad. "Tell me what you know of your people. You said you were two when the trapper found you? Was there anything on your clothing that told him of your tribe?"

The boy gulped down another bite. "The only band he knew of in the area where he found me were Peigan, but when he took me to the place they'd been camped, the whole group was gone."

She leaned forward. "Where were they camped? Do you know how to find the place?"

He nodded as he swallowed another bite. "I think so. It might be near where you're headed now. Pierre and I passed by there a few years back on our way through the mountains. If I could find those hot springs, I think I could find the valley where he said they were camped."

Good. There might be a real chance this boy had been a member of her band. Her memory was hazy from fifteen years ago, but she could remember more than one family mourning the loss of a child stolen by raiding war parties. It was possible this boy had been separated from his captors and left to die in the mountains.

She refocused on the lad. "Tell us of your life with Pierre. Where did you live?"

He had to swallow again before he could speak. She should probably leave him to eat in silence since he was shoveling food in his mouth as though he'd not had a meal in days. But he was already starting in on his answer. "We wandered the rivers mostly. Trapping. Usually we'd make a regular path through the mountains and back. That trip would take about two years. Sometimes we'd go farther north, and once or twice we went south, but the trapping's not as plentiful down there."

"Did you have a home at all?" Hadn't he mentioned a cabin earlier?

He shrugged. "A little place we'd stop in from time to time. Didn't leave our valuables there since others used it too."

A true vagrant then. Not a life she'd want to live.

The boy scraped the bottom of his tin as if he was determined to scoop up every bit of juice from the beans.

She reached for his plate. "Let me refill that. There's plenty here."

His gaze lifted to her face and lingered for a moment before he handed over the dish. "Thank you."

As she scooped more food, she slid a glance at Samuel. He'd offered to hold Cherry while she ate—almost insisted on taking the babe. In truth, she hadn't resisted much. Having a few moments with her hands free felt wonderful, even if that thought came with a nudge of guilt.

Watching him now, sitting cross-legged with the bundled baby tucked against him, sent a warmth through her that made her eyes sting. Such a large, strapping man, yet he looked so natural with the little one. And he seemed to harbor genuine affection for her daughter.

He was almost too wonderful to be real. The man could help bear not only the weight of their safety and the work involved in the journey, but with Samuel around, she no longer had to carry the full responsibility for her daughter's every need. For her very survival.

He looked up at her then, meeting her gaze across the fire. His eyes held their usual dark earnestness, but there was something else there too. A surety. A softness.

The look was almost her undoing. She blinked and dropped her gaze to the plate of beans. "Here you go." She handed it to Matisse without looking up.

She couldn't let herself weaken like this. She may have been fathered by a black-hearted French lowlife, but she was the grand-daughter of War Eagle. She wouldn't fall apart.

Not for any reason.

~

"What's wrong?" Samuel's pulse darted through his chest as he reined his gelding even with Mrs. Clark's mare. Her face had paled to a weak gray since he last looked at her. "What happened?" Had she seen something?

His gaze shot to Matisse, who'd been riding ahead and now looked back at them in question. The lad hadn't done anything to frighten her, Samuel was almost certain. He'd been watching the boy's every movement.

Samuel turned back to the woman, and the sight of her tightened the knot forming in his gut. Her lips were a brighter red than normal. "Are you ill?"

She looked at him, and her eyes didn't hold their normal intensity. Their weakness now sent a fresh bolt of fear through him.

Then she opened those crimson lips. "I'm well."

But she wasn't. She looked to be swaying in the saddle.

"Let me hold Cherry, at least." He leaned closer to rein in her horse as he did the same with his. "I should have offered this long before. It can't be easy to have her weight on you all day."

Thankfully, the horses stood still as he helped remove the sling and baby from Mrs. Clark. She winced as they worked the contraption off of her.

"You're hurt. What happened?" He took the baby in both hands, careful to support her little head. She was bundled so tightly, the blankets did all the work to hold her straight.

Mrs. Clark shook her head. "I'm not hurt. My shoulder only aches from the sling." She raised a hand to her left shoulder.

He should have taken the babe days before. Turning his focus to the sleeping little one, he fit the strap over his own shoulder. Once he was sure Cherry should be comfortable, he turned back to her mother.

She almost slumped in the saddle, a posture he'd never seen from her normally regal form. Her left hand rested in front of her, her right holding it in place as though the limb might fall away.

"Are you sure you're not ill?"

"I'm well." Her words held a prick of frustration.

He heaved out a breath. "Another hour or so and we can rest for the midday meal. Just call out if you want to stop before then."

She didn't respond, but her red lips had tightened into a thick line. Was she angry with him? Or trying to hold in whatever was wrong with her?

Either way, he'd be keeping a close eye on her. Something wasn't right.

~

*M*oriah could barely hold herself upright as her body shifted with the rhythm of the horse. The pain in her left breast was more excruciating than anything she'd ever felt, except maybe childbirth itself. What was happening to her?

The agony made it almost impossible to move her left arm or touch any part of that area. And now chills had taken over the rest of her body, along with an ache that seared all the way to the core of her bones.

She couldn't seem to stop shaking. If Samuel looked back again, he'd see it and make them stop. And maybe she did want to rest. She might not last much longer without losing consciousness.

Clutching the saddle tighter, she fought against a new wave of shivers. Her teeth chattered, and she tried to pull the fur tighter around her. The movement sent a fresh stab of pain through the tender flesh already screaming in agony.

"What's wrong?" The urgency in Samuel's voice nearly broke through the wall of tears she'd been holding back.

He was beside her a second later, his hand touching her good arm. "Look how ill you are." Then louder, his voice turned away, "Matisse, ride just ahead and find a place we can make camp. Somewhere sheltered from the wind."

Now his voice came back to her, deep and near. "Can you ride a minute longer 'til we find a better place to stop? This hillside is so open." She wanted to lean into his warmth, the strength of him, but she'd only fall off the horse.

Instead, she nodded, pressing her eyes closed as another shiver wracked her aching body.

"Mrs. Clark, I had no idea. I'm sorry."

His voice was the only warmth she could find, and she clung to it, even if only inside her mind. But she hated the way her surname stood as a barrier between them. "Moriah," she mumbled through trembling lips. "C-call me M-Moriah."

His hand slid along her arm, rubbing gently. "We'll stop in a minute, Moriah. Hold on a little longer, then we'll get you warm."

It seemed like half an hour before they reined to a halt, but surely it hadn't really been that long. She could hear the men's voices humming beside her as she sat atop her horse. Samuel and Matisse talking, but she didn't have the energy to push through the fog in her mind to understand them.

"All right, Moriah. Let's get you down, then tuck you into more furs so you can warm up." Samuel's strong hand reached up to grip her arm. But when he gave a gentle pull, the shifting in her muscles seared through her tender flesh at her side like a scalding blade.

She couldn't hold back the gasp, and she gripped her shoulder to keep her body from exploding.

"Is your arm injured? Where does it hurt?" Samuel's voice still held tenderness but now carried urgency, and maybe some fear.

"My shoulder." She gritted her teeth. "I can get down." Better she do this by herself to keep from jostling that side of her body.

He let her work at it, only settling his hands at her waist to help her slide from the horse. Then he led her with a hand at her good elbow. "Your pallet is right over here. We'll get a fire going soon."

"The baby?" She could only stand to focus on the ground right in front of her. The pain consumed everything else. But she had to know Cherry was being taken care of.

"She's snuggled in her blankets right now, still sleeping. I'll keep her with me as soon as I have you settled."

Samuel helped her onto a blanket, and it took everything inside her not to scream with the agony of using the muscles across her chest to lie down.

She was breathing hard as he pulled furs up over her. Then she tucked into a ball, curling tight to hold in any heat she could muster. Another shiver vibrated through her.

A strong, gentle hand rubbed along her good arm, and the touch was a combination of torture and blessed warmth. She ached everywhere.

"I'll be nearby." His voice was low, just above her ear, and she may have even felt the warmth of his breath on her temple. A tiny gift amidst the torment.

She squeezed her eyes shut. If only she could fall asleep and never wake up.

CHAPTER 12

"From torture to relief, my mind and body can't keep up."
~ Moriah

"Mr. Grant. You'll never guess what I found."

Samuel turned from the tiny flames he was kindling to see what stirred the excitement in Matisse's voice.

"It's a hot spring. Just around the side of this mountain." The boy lowered his armful of kindling to the ground near the fire. "I bet a soak there would warm Mrs. Clark right up."

Would it? Getting wet in this weather sure wouldn't help her, but maybe if the water was warm enough, it would help ease her pain and maybe even break her fever. He'd always heard the minerals in hot springs possessed great healing powers.

He turned to Mrs. Clark—Moriah. His heart stuttered as the name settled like a warm steam soothing his insides. It was strong and beautiful, just like her. The honor of knowing her given name, of being allowed to call her such, felt like a significant thing. But it wasn't an

Indian name, was it? Did she have a name in each language? Who had named her Moriah?

The thoughts fled as he took in her curled frame, buried under all the furs and blankets he could find. Yet still, her shoulders trembled. His chest ached as he witnessed her in so much pain. If there was anything he could do to take it from her, he'd do it in a heartbeat.

He settled a hand on her right shoulder, not the limb she said hurt so badly. "Moriah, did you hear what Matisse said about the hot spring? Do you want to try soaking in it?"

A murmur drifted from the opening in the furs. He leaned closer, stroking the coverings over her arm. "Was that a yes?"

"Yes." The word was muffled but understandable.

"All right then." He rose and looked at Cherry. He hated to disturb her again since she was sleeping so well, but he also wasn't ready to leave Matisse alone with the babe. If the lad did something to hurt her, even accidentally, Samuel wouldn't be able to live with himself.

He eased Cherry into her sling and slipped it over his neck. "Sorry, Little Bit. We're going for another ride."

As he moved back to help Moriah up, he noticed Matisse had taken his place building the fire. Good.

She seemed so weak as he helped her walk the short distance around the side of the low mountain where the lad said the spring lay. So frail. And he still didn't know exactly what was wrong with her, other than a fever. The pain in her shoulder was a mystery, unless the weight of carrying the baby had really been too much for her weakened body.

The strong mineral smell greeted them before they saw the steam rising through the bushes. The water was well-hidden, a little pool tucked in among bushy cedar shrubs and several large rocks. If it weren't for the smell and the steam, the place would be almost impossible to find.

When they reached the water's edge, the awkwardness of the situation settled over him fully. "Um...how do you want to do this?" Surely, she wasn't planning to dip in the pool fully clothed. *Lord, let her be able to handle the rest.* He wasn't sure he'd be able to maintain the distance he needed if she asked for his help to undress, even a little.

"I can manage from here. Just help me sit." She reached for the ground, and he lowered her with a hand on either side of her waist, trying not to disturb Cherry with the action.

Once she was settled, he sighed with relief and backed away. In the sling across his front, the babe shifted, yawning inside her bundle of blankets. He wrapped a supporting hand around her. Maybe, just maybe, she'd snooze a little longer and give her mama time to feel better.

He shifted his focus back to Moriah. "Is there anything else I can get you?"

She shook her head, huddled on the edge of the bank with the blankets pulled tight around her. "Just bring Cherry to me when she wakes up." Her voice was so weak, he could barely decipher it.

"I'll bring her if she needs you." The babe shifted again, her face contorting into silent complaint. He bounced a little to keep her quiet. "I'll give you privacy, but call out if you need anything. I'll stay close enough to hear." Maybe they should move the camp a little nearer this spring.

She nodded, and he slipped away just as Cherry let out a squawk.

The next half hour seemed to last forever. They did move the camp closer to the hot springs, since the fire was still small. Cherry was definitely awake now, and Samuel had to focus all his attention on her to keep her from crying, leaving Matisse to handle the rest of the work.

Cherry fussed and squirmed, and he laid her down to unwrap some of the layers from around her. Maybe she was hot. When he peeled back to the blankets closest to her skin, his fingers brushed dampness.

Oh.

His stomach churned, but he tried to ignore the sensation and focus on Cherry's sweet face while he worked. Except her sweet face was red and scrunched, and she writhed with grunting complaints.

"I'm sorry you're not happy, Little Bit. I'll get you dry as soon as I can, then we'll walk around and see what we can do to help."

He finally made it down to the bottom layer, a very soggy cloth wrapped between her legs and around her body. It looked as if it was meant to catch most of the messy stuff. Did Moriah have extras like this one? He was pretty sure he'd seen several draped over her brush shelter in the evenings to dry.

He hated the idea of going through her pack to find another cloth, but he also didn't want to bother her while she was trying to recover. There was a small satchel she usually kept with her when she was tending the baby. He would just check there, and if he didn't find it, he'd ask.

Inside the pack, the fabric he sought lay on top. *Thank you, Lord*. It wasn't as easy as he expected to wrap the dry cloth back around Cherry's trunk and make it stay, especially since she was kicking and squirming.

"Hold still now." Her skin was getting cold in the icy air. He had to bundle her back up.

Finally, he had Cherry snuggled in blankets again. She wasn't quite the neat package Moriah put together, but at least she would be warm.

"There now." He raised her up to examine his work. "You think that'll do?"

A glance at Cherry's face caused a laugh to form in his chest that wouldn't stay contained. Her tiny nose was wrinkled, and every bit of her looked so pitiful, yet cute enough to eat.

She loosed a gusty wail, apparently not liking his chuckle. He snuggled her tight in the crook of his arm and pushed to his feet. "I know, Little Bit. I get grumpy when I'm hungry, too."

How much longer 'til he should check on Moriah? The baby cried out again, this time more urgently. She wouldn't be denied much longer.

Matisse was working on the branch shelter they always built for Moriah and the baby. He was a good worker, thank the Lord. Samuel wasn't sure how he would've handled a sick woman, a hungry babe, *and* a diabolical prisoner.

As Cherry fussed and started into a steady cry, he did his best to bounce and soothe and slowly ambled toward the rocks and brush sheltering the pool of hot water.

"Samuel." Moriah's voice drifted through the foliage, and his heart did a skip at the sound of his name in her sweet, lilting tone.

"Yes?" He moved closer so he wouldn't miss her answer.

"Bring her to me."

He hesitated, a bit of relief warring with his urgency to protect Moriah. And Cherry, too, for that matter. Was her mother really strong enough to care for her?

"I'm better. The water's finally warmed me." Her voice did sound stronger.

"All right." He stepped toward the path through the bushes. But then he paused. "Are you...covered?"

"Yes."

He eased out a breath and started forward again.

She was sitting on the bank, her feet still dangling in the steaming water. A fur wrapped around her body, so the only part he could see was the elegant profile of her face—the straight, regal line of her nose and chin, her high cheekbones. Every beautiful feature working to form the entire masterpiece.

She turned at his approach, her gaze focused on the crying bundle in his arms. As he neared and crouched beside her, the fur shifted and her hands slipped through the opening to take the baby.

"There now. I'm here." The child hushed almost instantly as Moriah tucked the bundle against her shoulder. "All is well." A few hiccuping sobs shuttered out, but nothing more.

Moriah raised her gaze to his with a look so gentle it made his chest ache. "Thank you for taking care of us."

He swallowed, trying to force down the lump in his throat. "I changed her out of her wet things. I didn't know what else to do, so we've been walking and talking."

"That's exactly what she needed." Her gaze still bore the weariness from before, but a softness, too. A gentleness that made him want to draw closer. To wrap an arm around her back and maybe test those lips that called to him.

He forced his gaze to hold hers and not wander. "How are you feeling?"

The tired lines of her mouth curved a tiny bit. "Better, now that I'm warm."

"What do you think brought this on? Overtired?" Perhaps he shouldn't inquire about such personal things, but he needed to make sure this never happened again.

She hesitated. "I'm...not sure. I think the pain may be from infection. Perhaps the fever, too."

Infection usually came from a wound. "Were you hurt? Injured?"

She shook her head, hesitation again marking her movement. But she didn't say anything more.

He pinched his mouth shut. That must be as far as he should prod. If the issue was related to the baby, he was pretty sure there wasn't anything he could do.

Cherry squirmed in her mother's hold. A sign it was time he leave them alone.

Easing to his feet, he stepped back. "We've moved the camp over so we're closer to this pool. Call out when you need me, for the baby or anything else." He hesitated, letting his gaze run the length of her for the first time. "Will you be warm enough?" If she had wet layers under there, the furs may not be enough. "We have a good fire going. Actually, Matisse does. He's a good hand at setting up camp." He scrubbed a hand through his hair.

She offered a weak smile. "I'm glad. And we'll be fine."

He'd better leave them to it. But as he tracked back toward the camp, he couldn't help a final look back. The sight of her sitting there, so alone and vulnerable, raised up that lump in his throat.

She may be weak and ill just now, but she wasn't alone. And he'd move heaven and earth before he let anything happen to mother or child.

*T*he pain in Moriah's side was almost more than she could stand, and the red, inflamed flesh helped pinpoint the source of the ache that pulsed through that entire area. Cherry was so hungry, so Moriah had no choice but to let her nurse from the aching area, too. Even though every moment was agony.

When the babe was satisfied, Moriah managed to get them both up, then collected the furs and wet things. All strength seemed to have leaked from her body, and it took everything she had to walk back to camp.

She could do this, though. She would do whatever was necessary. She was War Eagle's granddaughter.

Samuel must have heard her movements, for he met her partway. "Let me help." His gaze roamed over her face, surely finding all the weariness she was trying to hide. But it wasn't disdain she saw in his response. Nor even frustration. It was more like...a yearning. A warmth that made her want to crawl in.

She'd never met a man like Samuel Grant. His kindness seemed to run soul-deep. But it was more than kindness. She couldn't quite put into words what it was about him that drew her. He was like a safe cave in a blizzard. A refuge.

She realized she was staring into his eyes and blinked, breaking the link between them. The weakness must be seeping into her mind.

"Let me take Little Bit." His low tenor slipped through her, and he reached out for the baby.

She handed her daughter over, and he peered into the blankets, then looked up at her with raised brows. "Sleeping again?"

Moriah tried to work up a smile. "I think you wore her out."

"Maybe you can both get some sleep." The warmth of his gaze caressed her face, but she didn't meet his eyes. She no longer had the strength to resist his pull.

Thankfully, he had mercy on her and turned toward the camp. "Come rest by the fire. You must be freezing. I have some corn mush heating if you're hungry."

They'd already built her brush shelter, so she draped her wet things to dry, then sank onto the blankets already spread out for her. She had to tell them to stop doing so much for her. She would carry her weight of the work around here.

She *would*.

But just now, they'd done it all. And she could barely hold herself upright on the pallet of bedding. She lowered onto her side, clenching her jaw against the pain radiating through the inflamed area. What could she do to make the infection go away? Maybe it would work itself out. *Lord, please.*

CHAPTER 13

"Every decision has consequences I never foresaw. Guide me, Lord."
~ Samuel

Oriah eyed Samuel as he lowered to his knees beside her, a plate in his hand and Cherry already positioned in the sling across his chest. As much as she would love to watch him with her daughter for the rest of the day, he shouldn't be burdened with the babe.

She patted the ground in front of her. "Lay her here with me."

"I will in a minute. Eat this first, if you can." He lowered the plate and held out a cup. "The water's warm."

"Excuse me. Mr. Grant? Ma'am?"

They both turned to look up at Matisse, who stood a few steps away.

He was holding out something in his hand, a small white object she couldn't quite make out. "I don't know if this will help, but Pierre always kept these around. When either of us was ailing, we'd eat one.

He called it garlic, and it always seems to help. Maybe Mrs. Clark would want to try one?"

Samuel straightened and reached out, taking what the boy offered. He held it between his thumb and forefinger, giving her a better look at the oval shaped piece that was half the length of her little finger and milky white.

The sight stirred a memory. Not a full recollection, just an impression. One of the older women had given something like this to her mother when she'd had a knife wound that festered.

She lifted her focus to Samuel, whose raised brows held a skeptical look. She nodded. "I think I know of this. I'll try it." At least, she prayed it was the same thing that had given her mother strength. She'd be willing to try almost anything at this point, except... She looked to Matisse. "Will it hurt the baby?" That should have been her first thought.

His brow puckered. "I...don't know for sure. It tastes awful, but it always seems to make us feel better in a few hours. I'd think if it doesn't hurt the rest of us, it shouldn't hurt the little one either." He squinted, as if recalling a memory. "I remember taking them when I had a broken arm as a boy, maybe four or five."

The apprehension in her chest eased some with his words. "All right." She reached for the garlic. "Should I chew it?" The thing was too big to swallow whole.

He nodded. "Yes, ma'am. You'll want to have plenty of water handy. It tastes bad enough to bring tears."

The boy wasn't exaggerating. As she chewed, she had to squeeze her eyes shut to keep from spitting the awful stuff into the dirt. The water did little to wash away the taste. She reached for the plate of corn mush, trying not to let her face betray the horrible taste. She could stomach it as well as any other man or woman, but she certainly didn't relish another dose.

She'd downed several bites before the spicy taste of the garlic lessened on her tongue. Laying the plate aside, she finally chanced a look at Samuel, who was still kneeling in front of her.

His strong face had softened in compassion. "Pretty bad, eh?"

She worked to keep a grimace from her face. "I wouldn't eat it for pleasure." She nodded toward the baby. "I can take her now."

He nodded and lifted the bundled infant out of the sling, performing the task with a smoothness that only came from practice. A knot of emotion thickened in her throat. He was so good with her baby. She hated that she needed so much help from him, but in truth, this man was a gift from God. It would be too easy to fall into his strength and let him take over.

But she couldn't do that. She had to get up and accomplish her own work. And she would, as soon as her weary body rested just a few minutes.

~

Samuel eyed Moriah's quivering back as she lay curled into the dark interior of the brush shelter. The fever must have returned in the hours she'd been sleeping. As soon as she finished nursing the baby, maybe she'd let him help her back to the hot spring. That seemed to have done a world of good for her earlier.

At last, she shifted, pulling the blankets around her as she curled tighter into a ball.

He didn't want to seem overly familiar with her, but she needed someone to take care of her with this illness. He wanted to be that someone. Stepping closer, he lowered his voice so he wouldn't wake the baby, who must be sleeping again. "Moriah?"

Her head lifted so she could look at him, but she kept the fur pulled up so only her eyes peeked out.

"Here's some warm water to drink."

She slipped her hand out the opening in the blanket to take the cup.

He crouched beside her, helping her grip the handle. Her hand was shaking so violently, water would have sloshed out if he'd filled it all the way. "Why don't you go back to the hot spring to get warm? I'll keep an eye on Cherry."

Her gaze lifted to his as she sipped the water. Even her jaw quivered from the cold.

He reached forward and rested the back of his fingers on her forehead. The soft skin was so hot, he nearly jerked his hand back. His chest tightened. "You're very feverish. The spring made you feel better before."

Those beautiful eyes had lost their strength as they stared back at him. Was she too weak to get up and walk to the pool?

"I can carry you if that's easier."

That seemed to push her into action. She placed the cup aside and worked herself upright. "I can do it."

She struggled to stand, and he helped her up with a hand at her elbow. But she pulled away as soon as she found her balance. After grabbing the shirt she'd hung up to dry earlier, she turned and marched toward the trail to the spring. "Call me if Cherry wakes."

Her brush-off shouldn't have bothered him. It was good she was able to stand and walk to the water on her own. Her strength must be returning.

He reached for his rifle, which was overdue for a good cleaning. Matisse had gone hunting, but with dusk settling so deeply, he should be back soon. At least, this would give Samuel something to do while he waited to see if he was needed.

Needed. He was a sorry excuse for a man sometimes. He'd always been a sucker for anyone who needed him, sometimes even putting his own life on hold to help. Like when Seth had become embroiled in the gambling den they'd managed back in Sacramento. Samuel hadn't liked the place from the get-go, but his brother had been so excited about the prospect of managing their own business, Samuel had agreed.

Then the establishment and the vices it encouraged had sunk their claws in Seth's throat, and Samuel had felt more helpless than any other moment in his life. He'd left the business—he couldn't stand another day in that den of iniquity, and he thought maybe Seth would join him on the ranch where he found a job. But Seth was bound too tightly to the vices that held him. Only God's grace had finally freed his brother from the addictions, and Samuel had been more than happy to hightail it out of Sacramento and head north for a fresh start. Unfortunately, he'd had to leave his steady job as a ranch hand behind.

He finished wiping down the rifle's works and reached for a bullet to reload it.

Leaving his job had been worth it to help Seth break loose from his demons. Seth had needed—

A scream ripped through the air, breaking his thought.

Strength surged through him as he snapped his rifle closed and bolted to his feet. That had to be Moriah. Had she seen a bear? A man? Had Matisse sneaked close while she was indecent?

The thought spurred him forward, rifle in hand, anger sluicing through him. He'd finally decided to trust the boy. If he'd missed a devious streak in the lad and Moriah was harmed, he'd never forgive himself.

Another scream, this time sounding almost like two different voices. Both high pitched and female—cries of pain. But how could there be two?

He charged down the path, breath coming in spurts as he raised the rifle to cock it. Thankfully, he'd had one bullet loaded when he heard the cry. *Lord, let that be enough.*

As he rounded the last rock that concealed Moriah from his view, the ruckus grew louder. Splashing and squeals and yelps. She must be fighting something off. "Help!"

He slowed enough to let his eyes take in the sight before him, which had suddenly stilled. Something big and long lay on the bank where Moriah had sat earlier that day. An animal? In the dim light of dusk, his mind had trouble placing the shape.

Then its massive head turned toward him, and an icy chill plunged down his back.

A mountain lion.

Where was Moriah? Her screams had ceased. He edged forward in a half circle so he could get a better angle at the cat's side, raising his rifle into position to shoot. But he had to know where Moriah was before he'd pull the trigger. Had she ducked underwater? Probably. That would be the smartest way to get away from a cougar. In this dusky light, he couldn't see beneath the surface to know for sure.

But what if she'd already been injured badly? What if she was, even now, drowning, unable to pull herself up to draw a life-sustaining breath.

"Moriah," he yelled. He wasn't sure if he wanted her to answer or not. She might call the cat's attention back on herself.

The mountain lion turned at his call, almost facing him, but still giving him a clear view of its heart. He should be able to make the shot, even in the almost-dark.

Samuel sighted down the barrel. *One bullet, Lord. Make it count.*

The lion crouched, preparing to spring. He pulled the trigger.

A flash of light exploded from the gun, and the cloud of powder blurred his vision of the cat.

A hiss and a howl sounded as the echo from the rifle faded. *The animal wasn't dead.* Samuel stepped to the side to get a better view.

The cat had moved closer to him. Still in a crouch, but now less than three strides away from him. Had he even hit the beast? That might be a bloody spot above its shoulder, but he couldn't tell for sure.

And now he had nothing to fight it off with except a rifle, which he could use as a club. He spun the gun so he gripped the barrel in both hands.

The mountain lion sprang at him.

Samuel struck with the butt of the weapon, catching the animal in the chest to slow the charge. At the same time, he stepped to the side.

One front claw swiped his arm. The pain barely registered as he swung around to face the animal again. The cat landed heavily on the ground, heavier than Samuel would expect from such a lithe, deadly creature. Maybe his bullet had done some damage after all.

But the animal didn't stay down. Spinning, it launched another attack.

He vaguely heard a scream as he swung the rifle again. His foot slipped on a wet rock as the animal slammed into his middle. It managed a hard paw to Samuel's side before he was able to push it away.

Another gunshot sounded. Another flash lit the darkness to his left.

The cougar fell in a mound in front of him.

"Matisse?" Samuel didn't dare take his eyes off the cougar, not until he was sure it wouldn't spring to life again.

"Here." The boy seemed to be breathing hard.

"Keep your gun pointed at that animal. I have to find Moriah."

"I'm here." The words came in the most beautiful voice he'd ever heard.

He searched for the source, his feet carrying him forward as his eyes tried to find her in the darkness. A ripple in the water guided his gaze. There she was, across the small pool and moving toward him.

He dropped to his knees at the edge of the bank. "You're alive."

Moriah's face was paler than he liked, but maybe that was the moonlight reflecting on the water. Her hands raised from the water, and he took them in his own. Hers were warm and supple compared to his wind-chapped, calloused skin.

"Are you hurt?" Her eyes seemed even wider than usual, tracking his face.

"Not bad." He could feel the sting across his side every time he drew breath, but he'd heal. "What of you?"

Then he saw it. She turned her face in the moonlight, revealing a dark line near her hair that stretched from her temple to her jaw.

"Moriah." He released one of her hands to get a better look. Blood dripped freely from the mark, running down her jaw, along the length of her neck, and into the water. He shifted back to meet her gaze. "Is there anything else?"

"Nothing. I saw her just as she pounced, so was able to move out of the way."

Thank you, God. He gripped her hand again. "Let's get you out so we can doctor that. Do you need a minute to dress?"

"Yes. I'll come to the camp when I'm done."

He hated the thought of leaving her alone again. "As soon as I retrieve my shot bag, I'll be standing right on the other side of that brush. Call if you need anything."

She squeezed his hand. "I'll be fine. Where's the baby?"

A knot tightened in his chest. Cherry was alone. Unprotected against any other wildlife that might present a threat. But he hated to leave Moriah unprotected, too.

"I'll stand guard." Matisse's voice came from behind them.

Samuel turned to see the boy still standing by the cougar's carcass as he'd been instructed. Even though the animal was certainly dead by now. "All right then." He extended a hand to the lad.

The boy hesitated, as if not quite sure what Samuel meant. Or maybe he didn't think it possible.

Samuel kept his hand out. "I owe you my life. Thank you."

Matisse slipped his hand into Samuel's with a nod. "Glad I could help."

Nodding, he released the boy's hand, scooped up his rifle, and sprinted back to Cherry.

CHAPTER 14

"This... How can this be?"
~ Moriah

Even before Moriah opened her eyes the next morning, a powerful ache pulsed through her entire body. Her cheek burned, but at least the place on her left side where it had felt like a knife was being twisted now only throbbed a dull pain.

A sound worked its way through her awareness. A low vibrato, almost a humming.

She pried her eyelids open and struggled to focus her sleepy vision. Beyond her brush shelter, Samuel knelt over his bed pallet, working on a bundle of blankets. A tiny leg kicked up from the cloths. A little foot she would never tire of seeing.

He was talking in a low murmur to the babe, his face animated with whatever he was saying. Those dark eyebrows rose and lowered with each expression, his eyes growing wide, then narrowing in a grin as a coo drifted up from the blankets.

No wonder Cherry loved him so. This big strapping frontiersman was willing to throw off his dignity to please a tiny babe. Moriah wasn't sure if she'd ever seen anything more attractive.

Samuel must have felt her gaze, for he looked over. A grin touched the corners of his mouth. "I was just changing her wet things and hoping she'd let you sleep longer."

He turned back to the baby and wrapped the blankets tighter around her, then lifted her up into the crook of his arm. He had a way of carrying Cherry somewhat upright, so she could see the world ahead of them. Probably another reason her daughter liked him. She hated to be held flat so all she saw was the sky.

"Here's your mama." He carried the babe over to Moriah and dropped to his knees. "How's your face this morning?"

She shifted so she could touch the cut running down her cheek. "It'll heal." Thankfully, the gash was near enough to her hairline that it wouldn't be obvious at first sight. "And you?"

Her gaze wandered down to his middle where he'd uncovered a gash from the mountain lion the night before. He waved the question away now. "I don't even feel it."

She met his gaze. "Make sure you put the salve on it this morning. Mountain lion wounds will fester badly without those herbs."

He nodded, giving her a pointed look. "You do the same." His expression softened. "How about the rest of you? Feeling better?" He reached forward and brushed his fingers across her forehead. Maybe he was only feeling for fever, but his touch sent a tingle all the way down her back.

She managed a smile. "I think so. I'll be ready to leave this morning."

His brow furrowed. "This is a good place to camp. Why don't we wait one more day?"

She shook her head. She couldn't be the weakling any longer. "I'm strong enough. There's no need to wait."

He tipped his head, studying her. But not with the intensity his gaze sometimes held. This look was easygoing and relaxed. "Tell ya what. Why don't we eat a good breakfast of cougar tenderloin, then see how everyone's feeling once we're up and around. If we want an extra day to enjoy the hot spring, we'll just take it."

She couldn't help a smile at his *cougar tenderloin* comment. And there was no sense in arguing with him when he was giving her a chance to prove her readiness. She'd just have to make sure she didn't show any more weakness.

Cherry took the moment to squeeze her face into a complaint, and Moriah reached for her. "She's hungry."

Samuel handed over the bundle, then pushed to his feet. "Matisse is checking the horses, but he left another garlic clove for you. And here's some water to wash it down. If that stuff tastes as bad as it smells, I don't envy you."

He placed the cup and plate beside her, then turned back to the fire. "I'm off to get more water for breakfast. Just call out if you need anything."

As he walked away, Moriah couldn't help the warm, protected feeling that slipped through her.

But as Cherry nursed, Moriah's mind churned forward to the journey ahead. They probably had only another day's ride before they reached her people. Then Samuel would leave her.

How in the world would she let him go?

～

A day later, Samuel eased back in the saddle as things finally started to feel back to normal. Aside from his raw wrinkled fingers anyway, a side-effect from washing soiled baby cloths in the spring that morning.

Never had he expected he'd be washing a newborn's laundry in the middle of the Canadian mountains, but Cherry was running out of clean cloths, and Moriah still looked pretty pale. She'd insisted she wouldn't hold them back another day, but if she started to look feverish again, he'd call a halt no matter how much she argued.

As his gelding charged up a rocky section of the trail, he wrapped a protective hand around the baby strapped to his chest. At least Moriah had allowed him to carry her for this first stretch. She'd have her hands full just staying in the saddle now that the terrain was more treacherous.

By the time they stopped for a midday rest and meal, Moriah's face had grown pale again. He settled her and the baby in as comfortable a spot as he could find, then turned to Matisse. "We should let the horses graze a little if we can find grass."

With both of them gone, Moriah would have a private moment to care for the little one. And grazing the horses would give them an excuse for an extended rest.

A little bit later, they sat in a circle, eating the last of the pemmican and leftover beans. Even cold, the meal satisfied all the hungry places in his gut. Matisse practically swallowed his food whole, a practice Samuel kept waiting for him to ease out of now that he had regular meals. But the boy never seemed to fill. Kind of like Rachel's son Andy had been on their journey northward.

He leaned back against a rock and watched Matisse stuff an oversized bite of pemmican in his mouth. "I think you've grown an inch or two since you joined up with us."

Matisse glanced up, eyes wide and guilty, as though he'd been caught stealing an extra bite of pie from the serving tin. Then one corner of his mouth tipped up. "Mrs. Clark's food is much better than Pierre's ever was." He slid a glance to Moriah as a bit of color filled his ruddy cheeks.

She offered him a weak smile. "I learned from my mother, who's full Peigan. She's the best cook in the camp."

A yearning crept into Matisse's gaze. "How many are in your camp?"

"About fifteen lodges most of the time. Maybe forty or fifty people." Her face softened. "My mother will likely take you in as another son. If we don't find your real family, that is. She's always caring for strays and anyone who needs a place to stay."

Matisse's jaw set in a hard line, but his eyes kept that longing, almost fragile expression.

They'd done a good thing inviting the lad to ride with them. *Thank you, Lord, for helping it turn out well.*

The boy pushed to his feet, maybe in an attempt to steel himself from a topic that left him vulnerable. "I saw a stream down the hill. I'll go bring up some drinking water."

As his steps faded into the distance, Samuel turned his focus to Moriah. "Do you recognize any of the land we're traveling through?"

She met his gaze. "I do actually. I remember riding through here when I'd hunt with my brothers." There was something in her eyes that drew him. Maybe the same longing that had been in Matisse's look.

"I'm sure you're looking forward to seeing your family again." A lump lodged in his chest. He didn't begrudge her the reunion, but that meant he would need to walk away. To leave her and the baby. Forever? He wasn't sure he could handle never seeing her again.

She nodded, then something shuttered her gaze. "What will you do? Go back to your family and Rachel?"

He pretended to contemplate the question, but really he was scrambling for a good way to ask if he could come back to see her. "I need to let them know about her brother's—I mean, your husband's— passing." Her jaw flexed when he stumbled through the words. "I'm not sure how soon they'll want to go on with the wedding. Rachel will likely need some time to grieve."

Moriah nodded but didn't speak. Was she holding in her own grief? He shouldn't have brought it up.

Now was a bad time to ask what he'd planned to ask, but this might be his only chance to talk with her alone. Especially if they reached the camp that night. "Once things calm down again, I thought maybe I'd come back up here and see how you and the babe are settling in. Would that be all right?"

Maybe it was his imagination, but it seemed as if her eyes took on a glimmer. Was that good or bad?

She nodded. "Cherry and I would both like you to come."

Some of the tension in his chest eased. "Good."

~

*E*xcitement had been building in Moriah's chest for hours now. The bittersweet kind, for she still wasn't sure how she'd handle Samuel leaving. But they were close to the camp now. Within the next few minutes, she would see her mother. And Grandfather. And all her people.

It seemed too wonderful to believe, these familiar landmarks they'd been passing as dusk settled. Each one brought back memories of a different lifetime. A past life she knew and loved, but one far distant from the world she lived in now.

And then the horses shuffled down an incline, winding around the massive boulder that marked the opening into the valley. Her ears strained for the sounds of industry that always drifted from the village. Even on a cold day like this one, the youngsters would be out playing. The thud of her beating heart must have been drowning out the noise.

She leaned around the boulder to catch sight of the lodges stretched out in neat rows. With each step, she strained harder.

But the teepees never appeared.

Had she fallen into a dream? A horrible nightmare? Where was the camp? Her mare stepped onto the level ground, revealing every part of valley in clear detail.

Nothing was left. Not a person, not even barren patches where the lodges had stood. As if they'd never been here. A numbness took over her chest, spreading up to her face. Clouding her mind.

"Moriah?" Samuel's voice barely penetrated her fog, and she couldn't find the words to respond. Her body simply wouldn't move.

All her plans—her only goal for months as she'd holed up like a prisoner in the little cabin Henry had built her—was to come back to this place. To reunite with her family, the people who would keep her and Cherry safe. Protected. She'd come so far. Finally reached her home.

Yet everyone had left. Abandoned her.

She slipped from her horse, then stumbled forward along the path that had been trodden so thoroughly, she'd have never thought grass would grow there again. Yet winter-brown blades crunched under her feet. The barren patches where each lodge had stood were barren no longer. The grass wasn't quite as tall as other areas, yet the land was reclaiming what it had lost, covering any evidence that an entire group of people—people she'd loved and sacrificed for—had lived and worked and thrived in this place.

She trudged down the first row, stopping at the third circle of shortened grass on the right. Her home for so many years. In the middle of the patch, she kicked aside grass to find the charred remains of what had been their fire ring. She couldn't begin to count the meals she'd cooked there. For Grandfather and the rest of her family and anyone he could coax in to join them for the meal. He was so well-respected, it was an honor to eat a meal in War Eagle's lodge. To eat of his women's cooking.

Dropping to her knees, she clamped her hands over her mouth, barely holding in the sob that surged up her throat. Why would they have left her? Where would they have gone? In her mind, she knew they'd assumed she was permanently settled and would have no need to return to their shelter. But couldn't her mother have sent one of the boys to tell her where they were going? Didn't she think maybe Moriah would need her, or simply want to visit on occasion?

But maybe when she'd finally wed Moriah off—to a white man, no less—she'd been relieved. Finally free of the burden cast on her by a hateful Frenchman all those years ago. Maybe she'd urged the elders to leave that place with all haste. To disappear into a land so distant Moriah would never find them.

She pressed her eyes shut, her chest aching as though a horse stood on it. As though her heart were truly breaking. She couldn't let herself slide into this pit, though. Her mother would never have left only to escape her tainted daughter. Moriah knew it down deep. She'd almost never treated Moriah like she wasn't wanted.

She had to focus her thoughts on something productive. Where *would* her people have gone? Surely not back to the place where they'd lived in the years before coming here. That had been a good camp with plenty of grazing for the horses, a regular buffalo route, and a hearty stream to supply them with clean water.

But then the white men had found their precious gold nearby and come in droves. Dirty, unshaven, ill-mannered masses. The place was no longer safe for her quiet people. They wouldn't have gone back there.

In the distance, a baby's cry drifted through her thoughts, so far away the sound almost didn't penetrate. She could keep her eyes closed and be back among her people, children laughing, babies making their needs known, women sharing news as they worked in the sun, tanning hides or preparing food.

The baby's cry grew louder, then a man's quiet murmur joined the sound. She forced her eyes open. She couldn't stay in that world, no matter how much she craved the peaceful haven. The safety she'd always felt there.

She blinked away the moisture blurring her vision. Samuel dropped to his knees beside her, his shoulder brushing hers. His presence eased over her like a warm breeze on a cold day. The baby lay in the sling across his front, her eyes wide but no longer crying.

A warm hand slipped around her shoulders. Steady. Strong.

Something inside her broke with the contact. She turned into him, the sob rising again. He pulled her close, and she rested her head on his shoulder, her face tucked into the crook of his neck. The babe lay between them, keeping her from hiding completely in his security. Yet she huddled as close as she could get. Craving his touch with everything in her.

Another sob broke loose, erupting from her chest in a jerky impulse. How long had it been since she cried? Not since Cherry was born.

And now... A hot tear leaked from her eye. She squeezed Samuel's arms, struggling to get herself under control. She couldn't break down. Not in front of him and the boy both.

She would find a way. She always did. And tears wouldn't help.

CHAPTER 15

"My heart breaks, yet the new mission fills me with relief."
~ Samuel

*I*nhaling hard breaths, Moriah pulled herself away from Samuel. He loosened his hold on her, but only a little. Enough that she could look up at him if she wanted to.

But she couldn't. Couldn't meet his gaze and see the sympathy there. Or even worse, the censure for her weakness.

Instead she focused on Cherry, who was staring up at her with those wide gray-blue eyes as though she were in the same trance that had overtaken her mother.

Moriah struggled to find words to say to her daughter, something to make this horrible dream go away.

Before she could speak, Samuel reached a finger up to her chin, tipping her face up so she had to meet his gaze. Those eyes, always so earnest, now had a glassy sheen. "We'll find them, Moriah. I promise."

The determination in his words, in those deep pools of brown, was almost enough to steal her control again. She dug deep, forcing her emotions aside as she focused on what he'd said.

"You'll help me?" Because she wasn't sure she could travel with Cherry alone. Not through the winter. What if she grew sick again? For weeks now, her daughter's life had depended on her alone, but she wasn't sure she had the strength to be that sole support any longer. Not in this cruel wilderness.

He nodded. "As long as it takes. I won't leave you."

As relief slipped through her, she let her eyes roam over his handsome face, soaking in the assurance there. The strength of his features. So capable of protecting, yet she'd never have guessed the depth of gentleness that lay within this virile man.

Was he the answer to all those pleadings she'd sent to God during the long nights with Cherry? Every time she was beset by lecherous men determined to take everything they could get from her, she'd begged God for help. Could Samuel be His provision for her?

A new awareness settled through her, sending a tingle to her core. She could love this man. It seemed almost irreverent to think it, only six months since Henry's death. And maybe the love would take time to strengthen, but he was more than she'd let herself believe possible.

She raised her gaze to his eyes again, a darker brown now than before. Without her consent, her focus dipped to his lips. She shouldn't be thinking this. Shouldn't be wishing he would draw nearer.

But he did. As though he could read her thoughts, he narrowed the distance between them. Close enough his breath warmed her face. Her eyes drifted shut as she relished the feel of it.

A baby's cry rose up between them, strong and insistent.

Moriah jerked back, heat flaming up her neck as she dropped her focus to Cherry. Her little face was scrunched, turning bright red as she complained.

"I'd better take her." Moriah reached to pull her daughter from the sling, but the angle was awkward, or maybe she was the one who was awkward. She couldn't quite meet Samuel's eyes, especially as he had to help her extract the babe.

"There now. Settle down." She raised Cherry to lay against her shoulder, swaying to calm her. "I think she's ready to eat. Where's Matisse?" Her gaze wandered past Samuel to the horses. A lone boy stood holding all three. "He must be disappointed too."

"Probably. I'll go talk with him. Shall we camp here for the night?" The hesitation in Samuel's voice drew her focus. His eyes showed uncertainty. Maybe he thought staying in this place would be too much for her.

She wouldn't break down again though. And this was the best area they'd find for hours. She nodded. "There's a stream just across that rise."

He rose. "I'll bring your pack and canteen. Take care of Little Bit."

As he turned and walked away, she couldn't help watching the strength of his broad shoulders. She may have set something in motion she wasn't ready for. But a strong part of her wouldn't have changed it if she could.

∼

Samuel kept an eye on Moriah as the evening passed. He'd never seen her look quite so brittle. She cared for the baby, but her thoughts seemed distant from this pleasant valley. Or…maybe they were caught back in a former time.

He'd wondered once during the journey here whether the people might have moved since she'd left them. But she'd been so certain, he'd pushed the thought out of his mind. Mentioning the idea probably wouldn't have changed anything. They still would have come to this place to see. Except maybe Moriah would have prepared herself for the possibility of an empty valley.

He could kick himself. It seemed like no matter how hard he tried to help, there was always something he missed.

Thankfully, the baby slept well through the night, only waking once that he heard. And he'd been awake enough to know.

His mind wouldn't stop plotting out the next step in their journey.

He'd put together a tentative plan, but needed to talk to Moriah this morning to see if she would agree.

Of all the scenarios that rolled through his head during the long night, this seemed the most practical and eased the knot in his gut that came with the thought of dragging her and Cherry deeper into the mountains with winter coming fast.

After the morning meal, Matisse wandered off to do some fishing in the nearby creek. They didn't have hook and twine, of course, but he said he could make a spear that would do the job just as well. Sounded like an arduous and frustrating task to Samuel, but the boy was welcome to try. He'd handled his disappointment over not finding the tribe with only a few words. Some time alone in this place was probably good for him.

Cherry lay face down on her belly on a blanket spread near the fire, Moriah sitting beside her. The babe kicked and gurgled, but her mother's gaze seemed to have again found that distant place and time.

He eased to sit beside them, then tickled the babe on her cheek. She cooed, a sound that never failed to pull a smile from him. He'd never have believed how quickly this little cherub could work her way into his heart.

In a selfish way, he was thankful the tribe hadn't been here. If they had, he might be leaving today. Even if he was gone for a few months, he'd miss watching Cherry grow into a rosy-cheeked toddler. Even now, he could see the difference in her over the last week. Her expressions were clearer. And she'd learned how to pump her little fists to show exactly how she felt.

He reached a finger to rub one of her tiny hands. "Have you noticed how she shakes her arms when she's happy or angry? One jerk means she's excited. But if she pumps them over and over, she's mad."

He glanced sideways to see Moriah's response. As he'd hoped, a tiny smile teased the corners of her mouth. "She's finding her personality."

"I think she's going to be a strong one." He wanted to add, *like her mother*, but he wasn't sure she was ready for that kind of compliment.

What almost happened between them last night might have been a surprise for her. He'd not expected the moment to turn tender either.

He still wasn't sure how things had changed so quickly. One moment, his chest was aching over her loss, determination surging through him to make this better for her. The next, she was gazing at his lips.

And he'd already been using everything within him not to look at *her* lips. That glimmer of longing in her eyes had undone all his restraint.

Then Cherry…

His body had rebelled against the interference, but it was for the best. Moriah had been through so much in such a short span. She needed time to catch up. His feelings for her felt like they were rooted deep in the very core of his heart. He wanted hers to be the same way.

Not simply an emotional response to devastating loss.

Anyway, for now he needed to focus on more practical details. He slid a glance at her. "Do you have any idea where they were planning to go next? Was there any talk about better hunting somewhere else?"

Twin lines formed between her brows, and she was silent for a long moment. "I can't remember hearing anything. I don't think they would have gone back to the place we camped before. It was overrun with miners, and much of the hunting was gone."

"Do you think they would have moved closer to the fort or farther away?" He hated to keep pushing, but he needed to know if there were any leads they should follow during the next leg of the journey.

"We were always peaceful, mostly trying to stay away from the white men. At least, until the last few years." A shadow seemed to touch her eyes. "I don't think they would have moved closer to the fort. Hunting and safety would be most important."

He eased out a breath. "Since we don't have a clear direction to start looking, how about we head south toward the valley where my family lives? I need to let Rachel know about her brother, since they're delaying the wedding 'til I return." He paused until she met his gaze. A fear had slipped into her eyes, and he tried to ease it with a smile. "And she'll want to meet you and Little Bit."

"I don't..." She hesitated, looking more uncertain than he'd ever seen her.

He reached for her hand and fit his big fingers around her slender ones. "They'll give us a safe place to catch our breath and restock supplies. I know they'll love you and the baby both." He willed her to see the truth in his gaze, to hear what he wasn't able to put into words.

She worked her lips, a nervous gesture and one that drew his attention where he ought not allow his gaze to roam. Then her focus shifted to the empty spot of ground where Matisse's bedroll had lain the night before. "What of Matisse?"

"I hope he'll come with us. It'll be his choice, but he's been a godsend. I'd hate to part ways with him now."

Her gaze searched his face. "Won't your people worry about so many strangers coming?"

He couldn't help a grin. "I come from a family of nine children, remember? This will just make the place feel a little more like home." Hopefully, they wouldn't overwhelm her, but he'd be there to help.

Her focus dropped to the baby, still lying on the blanket. "I suppose it would be good for Cherry to get out of the weather for a day or two."

A weight pressed his chest. He'd planned to tell her the rest of his idea, how it would be healthiest for her and the baby if they stayed with his family through the winter while he searched for her people. But right now, she looked like the mere mention of anything more than a quick visit would send her skittering away.

Maybe better to let her meet them first. See how accepting they were. How eager to take her into the fold. She and the babe would be safe there, but more than that, they would be loved and nurtured. Especially if his bossy sister Noelle had anything to say about it.

She breathed out a sigh. "I suppose we should go there. I owe it to Rachel."

He gave her hand a gentle squeeze. "We can stay here a few days if you'd like. That'll give you time to finish recovering from your illness. Just let me know when you're ready."

Finally she turned to look at him, all uncertainty gone from her expression. "I'm fully recovered. Tomorrow. We'll leave at first light."

~

*T*here was no rosy glow of sunrise the next morning, and Samuel eyed the thick clouds hanging low in the sky as he saddled Moriah's mare. He almost wished they were staying in this valley another day. They could build a shelter against the coming snow, and the horses would appreciate more time to graze in the thick grass. Too, he and Matisse could do some hunting. As it stood, they'd need to stretch their remaining supplies to make it to his family, unless they hunted along the way.

But Moriah was determined to leave this morning, and he certainly didn't want to prolong her sadness by staying here against her wishes. Maybe the snow would hold off a day until they made it out of the mountains.

He still wasn't sure which would be the wisest route to take. According to his best estimation, his family lived due south of their current position. He could lead the group southward and pray their path ran into the valley where they were headed. That would certainly be the most direct route—if he didn't get them lost.

Or they could backtrack to the edge of the mountains and follow that line south until they reached land he'd traveled on his way to find Henry. That would add at least a day, maybe two, to their journey.

He looked behind him as Moriah approached, the babe already tucked in her sling. Matisse trailed her with the two bundles he'd strap onto his own horse.

Samuel raised his brows at her. "Ready?"

Her jaw was set as she nodded, determination marking eyes still rimmed by red.

He held the mare as she mounted, reaching up to steady her elbow when she wavered. He knew from experience that mounting with a baby strapped to you wasn't easy.

Her mouth pulled in what she might have meant to be a smile.

Maybe he should share his questions about their route with her. Something to distract her, and she may be familiar enough with the terrain to provide valuable input. Matisse, too, for that matter, if he'd traveled as much as he'd said.

"I'm debating which way we should ride from here." He shifted his gaze from Moriah to the boy, then back. "I think my family lives almost due south of here, but their valley may be hard to find if we ride directly through the mountains. I know I can find it if we back-track to the flatland and follow the edge of the peaks, but that would add days. Are either of you familiar with the land to the south?"

Moriah stared out over the mountains around them. "We came from the south when we moved to this valley, traveling through the mountains. We accomplished it with children and animals, so the terrain is manageable. I may remember the valley you speak of, but I'm not certain."

A weight on his chest lifted. "That sounds promising." He looked to Matisse. "Have you traveled much through the mountains to the south?"

The lad rolled his lips under, a look that held more boyish uncertainty than he usually showed. "I can't say for sure. We moved all the time, and the land runs together in my mind. Maybe when I see it I'll remember."

Samuel nodded. He wouldn't count on that, but Moriah's words made him more hopeful. He looked back at her. "You think we should take the direct route through the mountains?"

She slid her gaze that direction, but her mind seemed far away. Maybe remembering her earlier journey? "I think so." The words came out almost wistful. Maybe the memories made her miss her family all over again. So much for distracting her from the sadness.

But then she pulled her focus back to him and offered a weak smile as she gathered her reins.

He gave the mare a pat, then turned to his gelding and mounted. "Let's cover some distance."

CHAPTER 16

"I never thought to feel this again."
~ Moriah

oriah had forgotten how treacherous the mountain terrain could be. That afternoon, the chilly breeze turned to an icy wind. She kept Cherry bundled in furs as much as she could, but it seemed impossible to keep the babe safe from the elements. Why had she ever taken her from the protection of the cabin? If they could just make it through a few more days of this, they'd reach Samuel's family.

A few flakes already swirled, and she had no doubt the thicker snowfall would be on them soon. Would Samuel keep riding or make camp early? She could ask to stop, but the farther they pressed on the better. She just had to keep Cherry protected.

The baby squawked in her wrappings. Probably tired of being so restrained.

Samuel glanced back at her from his place in the lead. His gaze searched the blankets, then lifted to hers. "We'll make camp as soon as we find a place somewhat protected." He scanned the rocky landscape around them. "I'm praying we find a cave."

A shiver slipped through her. A cave would provide good shelter, although the stone floor would be bone-numbingly cold.

Silence settled again as the horses picked their way over the rocky ground. Snow spun in earnest around them, biting the exposed skin on her face. Cherry fussed and kicked inside the bundle.

"Hold on, sweet one." Moriah shifted the babe's position to make her more comfortable. "As soon as we stop, I can let you move more." A little anyway. She couldn't let the babe be exposed to this chill. Already a film of moisture marked the delicate skin under her nose. What would she do if Cherry took sick?

"Look there."

Her attention jerked up at Samuel's words, her gaze following the line of his finger. She squinted against the snowflakes blowing in her eyes. Was there an animal traipsing along the cliff wall where he pointed? No, but could that shadow be a cave?

He turned his gelding that direction. "Wait here while I see exactly what it is."

She reined in her mare, and the yearling pranced forward on the rocks as Matisse reined in beside her. She tried for a smile to offer the boy, but her face felt frozen in a shiver.

Poor fellow, he looked just as miserable, hunkered down in his buckskins. He didn't have a fur at all. He must be frozen to the core.

"I think I have an extra wolf skin in my pack. When we stop, I'll pull it out for you."

He nodded, his chin quivering. He must truly be only half Indian, as his lighter coloring suggested. The Indian blood running through his veins should give him a higher tolerance for the cold, but not as much when diluted with European races.

Samuel had left his horse partway down the hill and now reached the shadow in the rock, his rifle in his hand. He moved forward into the dark place, disappearing as though he walked right through the cliff wall. It must be a cave. *Thank you, God.*

Her heart stuttered under the tightening in her chest as she waited for him to come back out. A bear or other animal might have chosen the cave to hibernate or find shelter from the snow.

She'd feel better when Samuel stepped back out, safe and whole.

A clatter sounded on the stones, like a herd of horses stomping. The noise was barely dimmed by the wind. She pulled her rifle out of the scabbard, although she couldn't shoot so close to Cherry. The noise would deafen the baby's ears.

"Here." She thrust the gun at Matisse, but he'd readied his own rifle. "Go help him."

The boy's horse surged forward just as shadows shifted on the mountainside around the cave.

Not just shadows. Bodies.

Mountain goats poured from the cave entrance, almost running over each other as they clambered along the rock face. She eased out a breath. Her pulse still hammered in her throat.

Cherry wailed, and Moriah bounced her to try to soothe. She didn't blame the babe for fussing. She probably needed a dry cloth and a meal soon, too. At least with the cave, Moriah could take care of her daughter.

Samuel appeared a moment later, a wonderful sight as he ducked out from the opening. The muscles through her shoulders and chest finally eased.

After clambering down the rocky slope, he patted his horse, then left him standing as he jogged toward her and Matisse. "It's a nice little cavern. Not too clean from all the animals that have stayed there, but we can sweep out a section. At least we'll be away from the weather."

They worked quickly, and within a few minutes, had a place cleared and the packs unloaded. Samuel knelt to make a fire while Matisse fed and tended the horses. She couldn't do anything but try to hush Cherry, who'd settled into a full wail.

"Go ahead and do what you need with her. I'll keep my back turned." Samuel raised his voice loud enough to be heard above the cries but kept his focus on the flame he was nurturing.

If she trusted any man to do so, she would trust him. And once she had Cherry in position to nurse, she could cover herself back up. The babe needed clean cloths too, but that should probably wait until the fire warmed the air that would hit her sensitive skin.

So she tucked herself into the shadows and finally eased Cherry's cries.

The blazing fire was starting to put out heat by the time the babe had nursed her fill, and Moriah took the chance to change the little one out of her soiled cloth. Samuel had a pot of water warming, which she used to give her daughter a much-needed wipe-down. If only she could do the same for herself. Maybe she could find a moment later if both men were out of the cave.

Snow fell in a thick curtain as Matisse tracked in and out of the shelter with armloads of wood. Samuel was tucked over the second pot warming by the fire, making the evening meal. A job she should be doing.

With Cherry bundled back up and propped where she could watch them, Moriah shifted around to Samuel's side. "Let me take over. I'm sorry I haven't been more help."

She reached for the spoon in his hand, but he didn't release it right away.

"I don't mind, Moriah. I'm not the cook you are, but I can make meat stew." His warm voice sent a tingle down her back, making her realize exactly how near she was to him. And the way he spoke her name made the word sound so melodic. Replaying the sound almost sent another shiver through her.

She inhaled a settling breath and nudged his arm with her elbow. "Go on, I can do this." She knew better than to meet his warm brown gaze. She'd get lost in him.

He released the spoon and eased back. "If you want to." Was that disappointment in his voice? She chanced a look at him, but he'd already turned away, pushing up to his feet. "I'll lay out the bedrolls so we're not sitting on cold rock."

An excellent idea.

Matisse came in with a final load of limbs for the fire. Snow covered his head and shoulders, and his skinny frame looked even more waif-like than usual. She pointed to the wolf skin Samuel had laid on her pallet of bedding. "Wrap that fur around you. I'll sew a clasp on it tonight so you can use it as a cape."

He reached for the pelt without arguing. A sign he must truly be in need.

Once the stew was ready, they all seemed to inhale the warm broth. Moriah let her eyes drift shut as the soothing heat soaked through her insides, warming every part it touched.

There wasn't as much meat in the soup as she would have put, but at least the stuff was hot. A thought slipped through her mind, and she jerked her gaze up to Samuel. "Are we low on supplies?" She'd packed plenty to reach her people, but they'd already gone farther than that and also added another member to their party—one who couldn't seem to fill the bottomless hole inside him.

Samuel kept his focus on his stew. "We'll need to hunt in the next day or two."

She studied him. "How long do you think before we reach your family?"

He turned to stare out into the falling snow, the white outside almost shimmering in the dim light of dusk. "I'm not quite sure. At least two days. Maybe three."

"When the snow stops, I'll hunt." Matisse didn't often speak up on his own. He must be gaining confidence with them.

She sent him a smile. "Good."

By the time they'd all eaten their fill, darkness had settled deep outside. The firelight lit a circle around them, cloaking them in a cozy almost-warmth.

Matisse stretched his legs in front of him. "I'll go check the horses."

Samuel gave a soft groan as he stood. "I'll walk out with you and bring in more water for the dishes."

Moriah eyed the pan of water she'd used to wipe Cherry earlier. This could be her chance for a quick wash.

The moment the men stepped outside, she moved into action. Within a minute or two, she'd cleaned up as much as she could and slipped into her buckskin tunic. Maybe she could heat some snow to wash her shirtwaist instead of traipsing back out to find the creek where Samuel was gathering water.

A sound from the cave opening made her spin. The man who'd just wandered through her thoughts stepped into the warmth of their little haven. The light from the fire lit his face, accenting each strong feature. Every inch of his rugged handsomeness. The breadth of his shoulders seemed to fill the cave, starting a flutter in her middle.

As he stepped toward her, his eyes took her in, and she couldn't help but flush. She hadn't wrapped herself back in her coat, and she was pretty sure he'd never seen her in her buckskins without the outer garment. Did it make her look more Indian? Did he disapprove?

Her heart picked up speed as he stepped closer, moving straight toward her with an intensity he'd never showed before. A deliberation that made her breath hitch. He paused a few steps away and lowered the pot to the ground, breaking the connection of their gazes. She inhaled a deep breath, willing the catch in her chest to ease.

Then he stood and stepped closer, bringing him within a stride of her. His gaze roamed her face, then slid down to her shoulder. He reached out and fingered the buckskin sleeve. "I like this." His eyes lifted to hers again, and this time they were darker than before.

She couldn't breathe. Every part of her responded to him in a way that almost frightened her. She'd never wanted a kiss as much as she wanted this man to take her in his arms and bring her back to life.

His breathing had turned ragged, filling the space between them. His fingers brushed over her arm, stroking upward. Over her shoulder, cupping her neck with a caress that sent another shiver through her. His hand moved up to her jaw as he closed the distance between her mouth and his.

Her eyes slid shut as the sweet warmth of him filled her. His lips were gentle, yet she could feel a strength in them that spoke of desire. As though he knew what he wanted. A frisson of fear slipped through her at the thought. Would he press his advantage, now that she'd shown her feelings? For she certainly wasn't holding herself back from the kiss.

Before she could process the thought, he eased back, brushing her lips with a final lingering caress. His hands cupped her face, and she took a moment to relish his touch. The security in his strength. The burn of tears crept in before she could block them. Why did they come now?

His hands slid down from her face, wrapped around her back, and pulled her close. Enfolding her in his strength, the solid security of him. She inhaled a shuddering breath, pressing her eyes closed so nothing leaked out. He smelled of man and woodsmoke and horse, a unique blend that was his alone, and it eased around her like a thick fur.

For a long moment, she let herself simply be held, inhaling his strength, renewing herself with his touch, with the steady beat of his heart.

Minutes passed as they stood there. She needed to pull away. To put some distance between them. To pull herself back under control.

He must have sensed her thoughts, for he loosened his hold, sliding his hands to her arms, then down the length of them to take her hands. He raised them to his lips, meeting her gaze with a tenderness that nearly unraveled her.

She almost turned away. Away from the earnestness there, but he still held her hands.

"Moriah." His voice was warm, gentle.

She studied his eyes, trying to see what lay behind them.

"This doesn't change anything between us." His gaze turned intense as he spoke. "I don't want you to worry. I may be falling for you hard, but you have to know that I'm still your friend. I'll always protect you. And I'll do whatever I can to find your family."

Maybe it was that intensity, or maybe it was his words that made her chest ache. She dropped her focus to their joined hands. What was he saying exactly? That she was just a pleasure he'd indulged in, and he vowed not to do so again?

I may be falling for you hard. That sounded like more than a temporary pleasure.

His finger touched her chin, tipping it upward so she had to meet his gaze again. "I *meant* that kiss. I just don't want you to worry or feel awkward around me now."

The way his eyes darkened when he said the word *meant* resurrected the sensation of his lips on hers. Something swirled in her chest, and she couldn't seem to stop her gaze from dropping to his mouth again.

He groaned and lowered his forehead to rest on hers. "Moriah. I've never known a woman quite like you. You may just be my undoing."

She wanted to speak, to say something witty, or to just prove his kiss hadn't stolen her ability to form words. But with the warmth of his breath caressing her face, she could do nothing except close her eyes and soak him in.

A whimper broke the moment. Moriah turned to where she'd left Cherry, sleeping inside her cocoon of blankets. The babe's face was screwed into the start of a cry.

She worked to disentangle herself from Samuel. "I'd better get her."

He touched her shoulder. "Let me. I haven't held that Little Bit all day."

As she watched him turn away and retrieve her daughter, Moriah had the feeling that—despite his words—things would not be the same between them.

Everything had changed. And that thought lit a candle of fear inside her.

CHAPTER 17

"Why can I never get it right?"
~ Samuel

Samuel breathed a sigh of relief as he stepped from the cave entrance the next morning. The dawn breaking on the eastern horizon splashed through the openings in the clouds. No more snow fell, although there was quite a bit covering the ground. The rocks might be treacherous climbing down from the cave.

Especially for a woman carrying a baby.

His body still came alive every time he remembered that kiss. Holding her in his arms afterward, he'd felt her vulnerability so much that his chest still ached for her. Maybe he shouldn't have pressed the kiss, but he'd seen the yearning in her eyes.

Still, in those few quiet moments afterward, he'd realized the depth of her fragility. For a woman so strong, there was something inside her so delicate, she raised every one of his protective instincts.

He wanted to heal her. To take away her pain and mend the broken places inside. But hadn't he proved himself no good at fixing people? He'd done his best with Seth. All their lives he'd tried to tame the insatiable thirst for more inside his twin brother. He'd never been able to curb his wild bent, especially not when the addictions took over.

And standing by to watch Seth's downfall had been the worst pain of Samuel's life.

Thank the Lord for stepping in. For healing Seth the way Samuel had never been able to. For bringing them both to a better place.

He squeezed his eyes shut. *I'm sorry, Lord.* Their Heavenly Father would have to be the one to heal Moriah, too. *Mend her wounds. Restore her to the woman You made her to be. And, Lord, I'm a willing vessel if you want to use me in the process.*

"You want me to hunt before we ride on?" Matisse stepped up beside him.

Samuel studied the sky again. The clouds covered about half the expanse above them but would probably break up as the day progressed. "I think we should start riding while the weather's good. We'll look for game along the way." If he'd been thinking straight, he would have brought down one of those mountain goats taking shelter in the cave. But danger had captivated his thoughts much more than the need for food.

"I'll go water the horses then." The boy slipped out before he could answer. Always staying busy.

Not for the first time, Samuel breathed a prayer of thanks for the lad.

Their entire group seemed to prepare slower that morning than usual. Maybe it was the cold. Or perhaps the snow added extra work.

Finally they were on the trail, with the yearling pouncing through the layers of white crystals like he'd never seen the stuff. The other horses plodded along, noses flaring when a covey of birds flew up from some bushes.

Samuel kept his rifle ready, but they never saw anything bigger than a white hare that dodged out of sight before he could aim.

Their stop for lunch was quick, mostly because snow covered

everything, making it hard to do more than stand in the wind as they ate.

When he finished repacking the leftover roasted venison behind Moriah's saddle, he turned to her. "How about if I carry the little one now that she has a full belly?"

She met his gaze, and it may have been his imagination, but her cheeks seemed to grow even redder than they'd already been from the cold. His heart panged. He didn't want her embarrassed around him. And he sure didn't want her to think he considered what had happened between them a light thing.

He reached out and brushed his hand down her arm. Through the thickness of her coat, she might have barely felt his touch. But he would show her in every way he could how much she meant to him.

The edges of her mouth tugged up, and she slipped out of the sling. "Thank you."

His heart lifted at the change in her, and even more when he took the wide-eyed cherub. "Hey there, Little Bit. You ready for a ride?"

A few hours later, Moriah took her back to nurse as they rode. The babe seemed to be eating more often the past day or so. That must be what it took to grow.

About an hour before dusk, he started looking for a good place to camp. It might be too much to hope they could find another cave, but if he could just find a rock overhang or a cluster of trees, they would stop. And probably too much to hope they could find grass underneath the snow for the animals to graze.

In this rocky terrain with cliffs towering on every side, there was little by way of shelter. At least, being near a creek was no longer a requirement. They could melt snow for water.

"Samuel?"

"Yes?" He turned in his saddle at Moriah's weary voice as they rode single file through a scattered line of massive boulders. His gut knotted at the weary lines on her face. Was her sickness returning? He should have stopped them long before now. They could use these stones for a windbreak and clear away snow from the ground. "We'll stop soon. In the next few minutes."

She nodded, then turned her focus back to the ground in front of her horse. This woman would soldier through anything without complaint. But he had to find a place for them to camp soon.

A glance at the sky made his muscles tighten even more. Low, heavy clouds had closed out the sun again. *Do we really need more snow, Lord?* They'd have to make a shelter to keep the weather away from Moriah and the baby. If not with branches, then with furs.

As the first flake swam in front of his vision, he spotted a rock overhang just ahead. The stone jutted about as wide as he could stretch his arms, leaving a section of ground with little snow.

That was better than trying to create a shelter.

Setting up camp seemed even harder than usual, what with trying to find enough wood to keep the fire blazing through the night and searching for fodder for the horses.

At last, they sat propped against the rock wall, Matisse on one side of the fire and Moriah holding the babe on the other. Samuel took his place beside Moriah as they had firewood piled on Matisse's other side.

He slipped his arm around her shoulders, and she leaned in to him. That act of tenderness—of trust—sent a surge of warmth through his chest. Cherry lay in her mother's lap, staring up at them with her big, round eyes. He reached out and brushed his finger down her cheek. It was red and wind-chapped, not the softness her skin had been before they'd set out on this journey.

"How's she holding up?" He raised his gaze to Moriah, her face only a handbreadth away from his. If she looked his way, he'd be sorely tempted to kiss her again.

She didn't. Instead she reached forward with a cloth and swiped under the babe's nose. "Her nose has been running since last night. I hope she's not getting sick."

A knot tightened in his gut. Cherry was still such a tiny thing. How could her little body withstand even a minor illness?

He had to get them to Simeon. There, they would have shelter and safety and someone with proper medicines and the knowledge to use them. His sister Noelle's letters had praised their oldest brother's abilities with herbs and other natural healers.

He ran his fingers lightly over Moriah's arm. "I hope there's only another couple days before we reach my family. We just need to hang on."

"I've been watching for landmarks I might recognize, but everything looks so different in the snow." She turned to Matisse. "Has anything looked familiar to you?"

"Same as you. It's hard to tell in the snow." The boy bit off a chunk of venison.

The sight of the meat must have brought his other concern fresh to Moriah's mind. She turned to look at him. "Will we have enough food?" Her gaze was troubled, worry darkening her coffee-and-cream colored eyes.

The knot in his stomach tightened. "We need to hunt tomorrow." In truth, they had enough to last only another day at the most. He'd eaten barely enough to dim the rumbling of his belly tonight, leaving the larger portions for the other two who needed food more. He'd do the same at every meal until they found fresh game. He should have allowed Matisse to take the time for a hunting excursion that day.

"I'll head out at first light." The boy spoke from across the fire.

Samuel leaned forward to send him a nod. "Thanks."

Then he settled back against the rock, letting his head rest against the cold stone. Moriah lay against his shoulder, and he could feel the working of her jaw as she ate her own dry venison.

He should have done a better job providing for them along the way. Maybe he should have insisted they go back to the flatland to ride south, where there might be more big game along the way.

No matter how much he tried to do the right thing, he always failed at actually helping.

He couldn't fail again. Not when the lives of this boy and the woman and child he loved depended on him getting this right.

~

*T*he snow wouldn't stop. All day, ever since they'd left the rock overhang that morning, they'd been riding through a steady onslaught of flakes. Moriah clenched her teeth against another shiver as her horse plodded along behind Samuel's. Each hour seemed colder than the last. She was hungry, exhausted, and so cold every part of her ached. Plus, she stunk of spoiled milk.

To make things worse, Cherry had fussed all afternoon. Eating wouldn't satisfy her, and her nose leaked like water in a loosely woven basket. Her cheeks were flushed, which might be from staying bundled up against the snow. But fear nibbled at the edges of Moriah's nerves. If Cherry was truly growing ill, what could she do? Was there a way to feed the child the garlic pieces Matisse had offered before? Maybe if she crushed them into a powder.

Would Samuel stop to camp soon? The sky was so dark, it was hard to tell the sun's position. Surely evening was near.

A few minutes later, he turned to them. "We'll stop for the night in those trees ahead."

Shivers convulsed her body, making every part of her ache as she climbed down from her mare. Cherry fussed and complained, but before Moriah could attempt to feed her again, she had to have a fire or she may just freeze to death.

Samuel and Matisse were removing packs from the horses, so she grabbed her flint and steel and some fabric shreds and birch bark she kept in her saddle pack. Using her feet, she cleared snow from the largest flat area under the trees, then dropped to her knees. She couldn't control the shaking in her hands, even with her gloves. But she wouldn't get warm until they had a fire.

The first strike didn't even summon a spark. Nor the second. With the third blow, the flint flew from her frozen hand, and she tumbled forward from the force of her effort.

"Moriah." Samuel was by her side, slipping his arm around her. "I'll do this. Sit and rest. Keep Cherry warm." He pulled her into his chest, wrapping both arms around her, rubbing her vigorously enough to stir her blood.

Her entire body shook, and his touch both soothed and intensified the ache in her tight muscles. He leaned back, and the warmth of his breath brushed her face.

He planted a kiss on her forehead. "Let me get this fire going, then we'll see if I can warm you and Little Bit up."

Cherry's complaints had risen to a wail, loud enough to scare off any game. Moriah had to tend her. If her daughter felt as awful as she did, the babe needed help. She turned to crawl to her, but Samuel stopped her.

"Sit. I'll bring her to you."

She pulled her fur tighter around herself, succumbing to the shivers. She wasn't entirely sure she could hold the child without dropping her, the shaking had grown so strong.

Samuel tucked Cherry in her lap, and she cuddled her, rocking. Trying her best to soothe them both.

"I'll work quickly." He pressed another kiss to her forehead, then turned to the tools she'd been using to kindle the fire.

Cherry's warm body was like a hot stone cradled in her lap, feeding the flames of worry in her chest. She needed to do something to help the babe, maybe try to feed her, but her brain felt like it was mired in fog. Every part of her ached from the cold so much she could barely move.

Finally, Samuel had a blaze growing, and he turned his focus to her. The worry in his eyes didn't make her feel any better. "Let me take her."

Cherry was still wailing, and Moriah let him extract the babe from her arms.

"It's all right, Little Bit. We're gonna get you feeling better." He used his soothing voice and raised the little one to his shoulder, her favorite position. The intensity of Cherry's cries lessened, but she still fussed.

He looked to Moriah and reached a hand to brush her cheek. "You're both feverish. I'll get the blankets out so you can lie down. Do you think she's hungry?"

"Don't know." It seemed like she'd just tried to feed her, but she couldn't think straight through the fog.

Samuel stood, and she curled into herself to find warmth. The hum of voices sounded above her, but she didn't try to make out the words.

The effort was just too much.

CHAPTER 18

"I hate this helplessness, yet I can't seem to control it."
~ Moriah

"I have a few garlic cloves left."

Matisse's words sounded from behind Samuel as he tucked the fur tighter around Moriah and the finally-sleeping babe. He rose to his feet and turned to the lad. "I guess we should give them to her. They seemed to help before. I don't know about the baby, though."

He scrubbed a hand over his face. He knew so little about doctoring, much less about how to tend a sick newborn. Moriah had said the baby was much too young to eat real food. Would the garlic—even if he crushed it—be too harsh for her tiny body? *Lord, show me what to do.*

Taking one of the small pieces from the lad, he knelt beside Moriah again. It was hard to tell if she was asleep or just exhausted. He placed a hand on her shoulder, and her eyes slitted open. "Think you can eat one of these garlic pieces?"

She lowered the covering from her mouth and parted her lips.

Those same lips he'd cherished only two days ago were now red and parched. Cracking. Maybe he could find a medicine in his pack to soothe them.

He placed the garlic in her mouth, and even though she was ill, the act felt so intimate. As she closed her lips and began chewing, he stroked his fingers across her flushed cheek, feeling the flex of her jaw. Her skin was hot, just like the last time when they'd found the hot springs.

"Do you hurt anywhere, love?" He brushed the hair from her temple.

"Everywhere." Her word rasped as though her voice were as weary as the rest of her.

"Like the last time? When your side hurt so much?"

Her face had twisted into a grimace, maybe from the taste of the garlic. "No." She spoke the word on a breath. "It's just the ague."

She made her illness sound like nothing, yet she looked completely miserable.

He stroked her forehead, smoothing out the grooves from her grimace. "What else can I get for you?"

"Water." Her eyelids drifted closed. "Just water."

Matisse had scooped a pot of snow to melt over the fire, so Samuel filled a cup and curled his fingers around it to absorb some of the warmth while it cooled enough for Moriah to drink. Was there anything else he could do for her? For either of them?

Show me how to help. Because what Moriah needed was beyond his abilities. Only God could fix the trouble they were in now.

∾

Samuel blinked in the light of morning, struggling to make sense of his surroundings. A weight lay on his arm, and he turned his attention to it.

The baby. Cherry lay on her belly in the crook of his arm, the blankets lifting where her little rump poked up as she curled her knees underneath her. A warm spot pooled in his chest, spreading what he could only call love through every part of him.

He watched her face for a few more minutes, the way her eyelids fluttered as though her mind were busy with a dream. Her tiny lips gathered to form a tiny O. Only the red circles marking each cheek gave hint of the long, frustrating night they'd had.

The babe's fever had kept her miserable for much of those long dark hours. When it became clear she wasn't hungry—just feeling wretched—he took her from Moriah and did his best to soothe, spending what felt like hours walking back and forth in their little camp. Every time Little Bit went to sleep in his arms, he'd try to lay her down next to Moriah, only to get a rousing wail as her face scrunched into that unhappy contortion.

Finally, he'd let her sleep in his arms as he sat on his own bedroll by the fire, praying for her healing with everything he had left.

A rustle lifted his focus toward their packs. Matisse sat on his haunches, his rifle over his legs as he hung the shot bag over his shoulder.

"I'm going hunting. I'll be back with food." He kept his voice low, but the determined look made his resolve clear.

"Take the mare Moriah rides so the yearling doesn't follow you." She wouldn't be going anywhere until after Matisse returned with food.

Matisse nodded.

"Be careful." He wasn't sure what made him add that. Matisse had proved himself capable. But as the lad stood and cradled the gun in the crook of his arm, his lean body still held the gangly look of youth, his tawny face smooth.

With another nod, the boy faded out of the camp, disappearing among the trees.

Help him, Lord. He's out of my hands. And that was probably a better place for the lad anyway.

Samuel turned his focus to Moriah, who'd spent her own restless night buried under the covers of her bed pallet.

Her dark eyes were open, watching him. Even sick, her beauty still had the power to bring him to his knees.

"How do you feel?"

She pulled the blanket down to her chin, so it no longer covered her mouth. "Better, I think." Her voice rasped, more than just the remnants of sleep. Another symptom of her sickness, most likely.

He shifted the baby so he could rise to his knees. "I'll get another of those garlics and some water for you."

"I'll take her." She shifted her covers again to make a spot for the little one.

Samuel cradled the exhausted little bundle as he knelt beside Moriah. "I'm not sure how long she's been asleep. Probably a couple hours."

Moriah raised tired eyes to him, the shadows underneath showing how much she still needed rest. "I'm sorry you had to stay up with her all night. I should have done it."

"No, you shouldn't have." He eased the baby into the place Moriah had cleared, tucked against her body.

His pulse kicked up a notch at his nearness to her. At the tender scene before him. These two girls had come to mean more to him than he was ready to admit. He reached out and brushed his fingers down Moriah's cheek. Her skin was so achingly soft, his callused hands were too rough to touch her.

But she raised her gaze to his again and gave him a weary smile that started his heart thumping anew.

"What else can I get you? Besides the water and the garlic." He would bring her the moon on a silver tray if she asked for it.

Except...he couldn't even make her breakfast. He swallowed the guilt that rose as bile in his throat. "Matisse went to hunt food for us." Because every last morsel was now gone. How had he let that happen?

She slipped her hand out of the covers and closed it over his. Her fingers were cold, even though her cheek still held fever. "I don't need anything. You've done so much already. Too much, but I'm grateful."

He couldn't stop himself from leaning forward and pressing a kiss to her forehead. "I'll do anything you need."

With every bit of willpower in him, he rose to his feet and turned to add wood to the fire.

It was time to put action to his promise.

⁓

*M*atisse still hadn't returned.

Samuel stood at the edge of the trees, staring out into the white wilderness around them. With the sun nearing the midway mark in the sky, the boy had probably been gone for five or six hours. Was game really that hard to find? Snow no longer fell, and the sky held more clear blue than clouds, which allowed the sun to beat with intensity. Surely Matisse would have found at least a couple of animals that would fill their bellies today. He'd proven himself a decent shot, so that shouldn't be the problem.

Samuel tried not to let his mind wander to what may have delayed the lad. Maybe he shouldn't have let him go alone. A fifteen-year-old in this snow-covered mountain wilderness? Any number of catastrophes might have waylaid him. Hungry mountain lions were surely lurking about. His horse may have fallen on the icy rocks. An accident with the gun was always possible.

Why had he let him go without asking more questions about where he planned to hunt? He should have warned the boy not to be reckless on the ice-and-snow-covered terrain. Every lad needed reminders like those.

At least, Samuel and his brothers had.

He turned back toward the camp and grabbed two more logs from their dwindling pile to lay on the fire.

Moriah sat up on her bed pallet, and her eyes looked brighter than they had that morning. She had a blanket draped over her front, which meant she was probably nursing the babe.

She offered him a smile as he crouched by the fire to position the logs. "No sign of Matisse yet?"

"No." His voice came out harsher than he meant it to. He eased out his frustration in a long breath. "I should have asked more questions before I let him go. I don't even know where to look for him."

"He's capable. Maybe he had to travel far to find game." A hopeful note tried to rise above the rasp in her voice. At least she didn't seem offended by his tone.

A new thought slipped in, building into a powerful punch as he mulled it over. What if Matisse had left them for good? Taken their horse and set out on his own again. He pressed his eyes shut. *No, Lord.*

Had the lad taken any supplies? Not that he could remember, but he'd not seen the saddled horse to know for sure. He spun around to where they'd laid the packs. The boy's bedroll was still there.

Good. He forced himself to take steady breaths. Matisse had been nothing but helpful, and they'd been kind to him in return. There was no reason for him to steal away and abandon them.

He shifted the pot of water so it wasn't in the line of smoke from the fire. Moriah needed to take another chunk of garlic. He had nothing else to offer her, but this did seem to be helping.

When he stole a glance her way, she met his gaze with a look that seemed to overflow with a sad kind of wisdom borne of hard experience. She leaned forward a little, holding his gaze with hers. "If you need to go look for him, Samuel, do it."

His chest clenched, locking down his breathing. He couldn't leave her and the baby, not with them both sick. But what if Matisse was hurt out there? He couldn't leave the boy to die in the elements, either.

What do I do, God? His spirit cried heavenward even as his gaze was held captive by Moriah's.

"I can't leave you and the baby." Each shallow breath was a labor through the worry clenching his chest.

The tendons in her jaw flexed. "We'll be fine. I'm better now. I took care of her alone before, and I can do it again."

He rose and dropped to his knees in front of her. "Moriah. You're not alone anymore. I want to be by your side. Working together. Here to help when you need me. Every time." If her hands weren't under the blanket, he would have taken them in his. Anything to make her see how earnest he was.

Instead, he had only his gaze and his words.

Her jaw shifted again, as though she were clenching against a war waging inside her. At last, her eyes softened. Even...was that a glimmer of tears?

He reached out and cradled her cheek with his hand. "You only have to let me."

The delicate lines of her jaw shifted again, but more like she was swallowing down emotion, not holding back anger. She nodded, then pressed her lips together. From the red tinging her eyes, that was probably another effort to stem tears.

She tried to be so strong.

He stroked her cheek with his thumb, and she finally seemed to pull herself together enough to speak. "Thank you. I do think you should go look for him. He's just a boy. Maybe he needs help." Her words were soft, almost pleading.

Digging down to chip away at his resolve.

He sat back on his heels and blew out a breath. "I can't leave you here with no food. What if something happens to me and I don't make it back?" The thought of her sitting here with Cherry, both of them sick and slowly starving to death, was enough to firm up all his determination.

"Samuel, I have a rifle, too." Her voice was so gentle, it almost soothed the edges of his fear. "If you're not back by tomorrow morning, I'll set traps and hunt around here. I know how to feed myself in the wilderness. It's been ingrained in me since I was old enough to walk."

She probably knew a great deal more than he did, but the weather... And she was ill. And she had a baby to tend.

"The sooner you go, the sooner you'll be back. And the better your chances of helping Matisse before it's too late. Take things to build a fire in case you have to stay out overnight."

God, what do I do? She was right. He knew she was. He should leave now and be back in a few hours. Hopefully, with Matisse and a deer or elk for their dinner. Maybe the animal was so big, the lad was having trouble loading it onto his horse.

He focused on Moriah again, studying her face for signs that she was too ill to be left. If anything, more color seemed to have returned to her face.

He released another breath. "All right. I'll saddle up and leave now. What else can I get you before I go?"

Her mouth curved up in a gentle smile. "Just come back to me."

If she wasn't so ill, he would lean forward and kiss her. Instead, he poured all his love into his words. "I will. No matter what. I will."

CHAPTER 19

"God, no!"
~ Samuel

The sun shone brilliantly as Samuel followed the tracks left by Matisse's horse, winding along the valley where they'd camped, then up and over the cliff to the east. The higher he climbed, the fiercer the sun's rays until he could barely do more than squint.

But he had to keep his eyes open to watch for tracks. Through the rocky sections, it was easy to lose the trail the boy had traveled. Samuel had to focus. A few other animal tracks marred the snow, and he might even find game along the way if he kept his eyes open.

He pushed his gelding as fast as he dared. Urgency squeezed his chest, tightening all his muscles and pushing his horse to go faster. If Matisse or the animal were injured or—God forbid—killed, Samuel would be leaving both Moriah and the lad unprotected. It might even spell a death sentence for them all.

The first peak he crested merged with another mountain partway down, and he slowed his gelding to climb the rocky surface of the second crest. The sun seemed to grow brighter with each upward step.

When he reached the top, a motion down the other side caught his focus. He squinted, trying to focus in the blinding glare of the sun on millions of snow crystals. Was the movement he'd seen merely a trick of his eyes?

No. There it was again, a dark figure. He reined his gelding that direction, and as he closed the distance, the figure morphed into multiple brown and gray shapes.

Deer? No, smaller than that.

Mountain goats.

He reached for his rifle. This was the part he always hated—taking an innocent life. But Moriah had to eat. They all did.

He tried to edge his gelding nearer the animals to clear the blurry haze from sun on snow, but the herd shifted away. He'd have to take a shot now or lose them completely.

Guide the bullet, Lord. Aiming as best he could, he squeezed the trigger.

The blast ripped through the still mountain air, scattering the herd in the midst of frantic bleats. He nudged his horse forward to see if his shot had hit a mark.

Yes. They could eat now. Hopefully this would last the day or two until they reached his family.

After draining the blood, he wrapped the carcass and strapped it on behind his saddle. Now if he could just find Matisse, they could go back to Moriah and little Cherry.

After mounting again, he reined his gelding back up the hill to the spot where he'd left Matisse's trail. His eyes stung from keeping them open against the blinding sun, but he had to watch closely to find, then follow, the tracks. At least it wasn't snowing, and the wind wasn't strong enough to blow away the prints. Not completely, anyway.

He spotted the trail and followed it. When he'd descended to the base of that mountain, he tried to gauge how long he'd been gone by the position of the sun. Two hours? Three? His head ached from the brilliant rays, both from the huge ball of fire in the sky and the beams magnified by reflection on the snow.

He had to move faster now. If he found Matisse this very moment, it'd be at least another two or three hours back to Moriah. She may be in desperate need by then. Didn't fevers usually worsen in the evening hours? Whatever happened, he couldn't leave them alone through the night.

There were likely very hungry animals lurking around. Mountain lions or wolves who were having just as much trouble as he'd had finding smaller prey in the snow.

He couldn't leave Moriah and that tiny baby alone—sick and at the mercy of anything that came for them.

Through the narrow valley, the wind kicked up into fierce gusts, blowing through the narrow channel between the mountains like a rushing train. Matisse's tracks disappeared completely, and Samuel had to ride along the base of the opposite cliff before he finally picked up the trail again.

Where is he, Lord? Show me. Anxiety pressed hard on his chest, making him urge the horse faster up the mountain. The higher they climbed, the fiercer the sun's rays beat down. His head pounded like the steady blows of a man and an ax splitting wood inside his skull.

This mountain was taller than the others he'd crossed that day, and when he finally crested the peak, he reined in his gelding to let the animal catch its breath. In truth, Samuel was breathing hard, too. As much from the weight on his chest as from the exertion of urging the horse up the mountain.

The sight before them was different than the terrain he'd been traveling, and it took a moment for his weary eyes to make sense of what he saw. Partway down this slope, a line of tall lodge-pole pines started, spreading down beyond the base of the hill. Then the ground leveled off into flat land for a stretch, rolling into gentle hills. Had he reached the edge of the mountain country?

A tall structure in the distance caught his gaze. Covered in snow, the spectacle looked different than it had the last time he saw it. A tall butte, standing higher than the tallest lodge-pole pine, with a huge boulder almost covering the flat top. It was as though the ground had washed away all around and that massive rock was the only thing that kept its platform in place.

He'd seen that boulder-topped butte on his way to find Henry. Late in the afternoon on the first day of his journey.

Simeon and the rest of his family were only a day's ride from here. Excitement surged in Samuel's chest, easing some of the pressure inside him. *They were so close.*

He nudged his gelding down the slope, and the horse must have felt his eagerness, for he had to rein the animal in so they didn't tumble head-over-heels down the mountain.

He'd almost forgotten to watch for Matisse's tracks until a deep indention in the snow made him pull the horse up short. The white fluff was churned in a section twice the width of a horse, running down the mountain for about twenty strides. Almost to the grove of trees.

Bile churned in his gut. Was this what had happened to Matisse? But where was the lad?

He pushed his gelding forward, scanning the trees for signs of motion. "Matisse!"

Maybe he'd taken shelter in the woods. And his horse?

No response sounded, but with the creak of Samuel's saddle and the shuffle of his horse's hooves in the snow, a call may be drowned out.

As he neared the woods, he could see a line pressed in the snow, like something being dragged toward the trees. He jumped from his gelding at the edge of the grove and squinted to adapt his eyes to the dimmer lighting. Flashes of light shot through his vision, almost blinding him for a moment as his eyes adjusted.

"Here." A voice—low and raspy—jerked his attention downward.

Matisse lay in the snow, tousled and looking so small wrapped in the fur he usually wore as a cape.

"Matisse." He scrambled toward the boy and dropped to his haunches beside him. "What happened? Are you hurt?" He scanned the length of the lad, then looked back at his face.

Pain scrunched his features. "Horse fell. My leg. And arm."

Samuel examined both his legs, and the knot in his gut tightened when he saw how big around the right thigh had grown. He shifted toward it and reached out to touch gingerly.

"Don't." Matisse bit the word through clenched teeth, his breathing growing heavier. "I already know it's broken. The arm, too."

Samuel turned his focus to the arm. He'd need to see the leg before he attempted to splint it, but he could wait a minute until he knew what shape the other limb was in.

Matisse lifted the gray fur from his right arm. The buckskin sleeve was pulled tight with the swollen limb inside, and a large bump protruded on the side of the upper arm. The bone below that bulge lay at an odd angle.

Samuel's gut churned. This was a bad break. The boy would be lucky if the bone wasn't protruding through the skin. He couldn't splint that kind of break, not out here in the snow and freezing cold.

And he couldn't move Matisse without securing the broken limbs. Even with splints, the lad couldn't sit atop a horse with his thigh bone broken. Not only would the pain be excruciating, there was no telling what further damage would be done by the curve of the saddle and the jostling of the animal's gait.

He turned to look up the mountain. He had no choice but to go retrieve Moriah and the baby, then bring them back to Matisse. None of them could be left alone for long, and all needed food and warmth.

Looking back at the boy, Samuel studied his face again. The lad shivered, and a sheen of sweat glistened over his features. The perspiration could be from pain, as could the unusual rosy blush on his cheeks. The shivering could be from lying in the snow.

But something inside Samuel told him there was more. He removed his glove and pressed a palm to the lad's forehead.

Hot. Was this his body's reaction to all the trauma? Or had Matisse contracted the same sickness Moriah and the baby suffered from?

Either way, he needed help.

Standing, Samuel moved around to the lad's other side and kicked snow away from an area that would work for a small fire. Thank God he'd brought flint, steel, and tender to build a fire. There were plenty of cured pine branches lying on the ground throughout the little glade. If he could find some that weren't soaked through, he could get a good fire started.

It seemed like hours, but he finally had a small blaze going, a spit of goat's meat roasting over the flame. The fire, the meat, and the extra wood were all within Matisse's reach so he could eat when the food was ready and keep himself warm for the next few hours.

Samuel dropped to his haunches by the lad again. "Anything else you need before I go?"

Matisse gave a single, painful shake of his head. His breathing had grown even more ragged than before.

Samuel scanned the area again. "Any idea where your horse is? I assume your rifle's still in the scabbard." He hated to leave the lad without defense against hungry wildlife. He could follow the horse's tracks to find the gun, but he didn't have time right now. He had to get back to Moriah.

"Don't know." The words seemed to be dragged from the boy's throat.

Samuel brushed Matisse's face again, then fought a cringe at the heat emanating from his skin. "It'll probably be five or six hours before I come back, but I *will* be back."

He was pretty sure he could manage the trail in the dark, especially since the moon wouldn't be hidden by clouds.

Lord, let Moriah and Cherry be able to travel. He couldn't even think about what he'd do if they weren't.

With a last farewell, he mounted his gelding and turned the animal up the mountain.

Praying with every stride this goodbye wasn't final.

~

Night hung thick around Moriah as she clutched Cherry, rocking forward and back. The baby was restless, but nothing compared to the turmoil in Moriah's own chest.

Where was Samuel?

Had he found Matisse, and whatever trouble delayed the lad was too much even for Samuel to overcome? She'd promised to go after him in the morning if he didn't return by then, but a part of her wanted to find him *now*.

What if another mountain lion had attacked? Or they'd run into someone who didn't like the color of Matisse's skin? Of course Samuel would do what it took to save the boy.

But maybe they both needed help. How many more hours until dawn? Four? Five? She would pack up the camp now and follow him if she didn't need light to find his tracks.

Cherry whined, scrunching her face and kicking inside her blankets. Moriah forced herself to relax. "It's all right, sweet one. He'll be back soon. They'll both come, and everything will be fine."

She lifted the babe to feel Cherry's forehead with her cheek. Still a little feverish. The garlic seemed to have cleared away the worst of Moriah's own sickness. Maybe she should have given it to her daughter, too. It was so hard to know what was best.

A shuffling sounded in the distance, and she sat up straight, straining to see into the darkness. Cherry's complaint changed to a wail, and Moriah bounced her as she struggled to stand. "Hush, sweet one."

She glanced to the rifle on the ground beside her, but she couldn't shoot the gun with the babe in her arms. If she put Cherry down, though, her cries would rise in earnest.

"Moriah, it's me. Are you there?" Samuel's voice sounded through the night, a distance away. Maybe from the edge of the trees.

Her body slackened as fear eased out of her, and she had to lock her knees to keep from falling. "I'm here."

The noise grew louder as Samuel neared. When he stepped into the firelight leading his horse, the sight of him stirred such a torrent of emotions inside her, she almost went down again.

He strode right to her, catching his arm around her and pulling her close, locking her and Cherry in the protection of his embrace. She laid her head on his shoulder, breathing him in. Soaking in his warmth and steadiness and...love. She couldn't find another word that summed up the gentle intensity of his touch.

Even Cherry was soothed by his nearness, for she didn't even squirm as she was tucked between them.

He drew back, and she had to stop herself from clutching at him to keep him close. But he didn't remove his arms from around her. Instead, he lowered his mouth to hers, kissing her as though he'd thought he would never see her again.

CHAPTER 20

"Let this be the worst, Lord. Please."
~ Moriah

$\mathcal{M}$oriah inhaled him, giving back as much as he gave. Pouring into her kiss all her relief and the wealth of emotions growing in her heart for this man. How could she not love him? He'd been everything she needed. Protecting, providing, caring…for both her and Cherry.

He finally pulled back, his breathing ragged. "Moriah." He spoke her name as though she were water and he were dying of thirst. At some point, he'd brought a hand around to cup her neck, and his thumb now stroked her jaw. "Are you all right? What about Cherry?"

His eyes searched hers, then roamed her face.

"We're better. She's still peevish, but recovering, I think. What of Matisse?" She looked over his shoulder. "Is he putting away the horses?" But Samuel's horse stood behind him, its weary head lowered in exhaustion.

Fear lit in her chest again as she looked back at Samuel. "Where is he?"

"He's hurt. Broken arm and leg. I couldn't move him. Do you think you can travel?" He peered down in the blanket. "How about you, Little Bit? Want to go for a horse ride?"

"Of course. I've already packed what I could. I was only waiting until daylight before I came to find you." She turned away to lay the baby down so she could start rolling her blankets.

"I brought meat. It'll be about three or four hours to get to Matisse, especially in the dark. Do you want to cook it so you can eat on the way?"

Her belly was so ravenous, it felt like her stomach was eating her insides, but that was nothing compared to the pain Matisse must be in. "I can wait. Let's get to him first."

~

Samuel blinked his eyes to clear them, but that no longer seemed to work. Was he so weak now that he couldn't stay awake all night without his eyesight going blurry from lack of sleep? The howling wind was making tears leak down his face, too.

At least they were climbing the last cliff before they reached Matisse. Surely this night would end soon, and daylight would aid them.

He squinted and used his coat sleeve to clear the moisture from his eyes again, then looked back to check on Moriah. She sat in her saddle, hunched against the wind, but he couldn't quite make out her face. The blurry form of the yearling tagged along beside her, keeping close.

"You need anything?" He called loudly above the wind. "We should see the trees where I left him over this rise."

"Good." Was that the chattering of her teeth that made the word stutter?

Maybe he should ride with her to conserve body heat. Although the two of them and the baby may be too much for either of the horses on this mountain. His gelding had already made the trip twice more today. And they would be there within the half hour, Lord willing.

He turned forward again to check the trail they followed, then gave his horse a pat on the shoulder. "You're doing good, boy."

The motion shifted Cherry, who hung in the sling at his chest, buried under his coat and an extra fur. He rested his hand beneath the bump she formed and lifted her slightly so he could see under the pelt.

She slept, but her breath rasped and her cheeks still wore the rosy rings of a flush. Maybe she was too warm under all the covers, but being exposed to this icy wind wouldn't be good for her either.

Protect her, Lord. Cradle her little body in Your hands and make her well.

At last, they crested the hill and started down the other side. Samuel motioned toward the trees. "He's just inside those woods." He wanted to loosen his gelding's reins and let the horse surge down the embankment, but he couldn't leave Moriah. Would Matisse still be alive? Samuel couldn't see even a flicker of light left from the campfire.

"Go to him. Don't wait for me."

He turned to look at her, studying her face to see if he'd heard right. Except with his blurry vision, he could only make out the outline of her fur-wrapped shape.

"Go." This time her command was clearly discernable.

He gave the gelding his head, holding enough tension on the reins to help keep the animal from falling in the thick snow of the downward slope. That must have been what happened with Matisse's horse, and the last thing they needed was two of them laid up with broken bones.

And he had to protect Cherry. He moved one hand to cradle the baby close as the horse's stride bobbed.

Finally he reached the trees. "Matisse." He didn't stop to wait for a reply, just slid from his horse and charged toward the place he'd left the lad.

Matisse was still there, but the coals from the fire no longer glowed. With one hand holding Cherry secure, Samuel dropped to his knees beside the blurry form that was the boy.

"Are you awake?" He jerked off his glove and fumbled for the lad's forehead, and a wash of relief slipped through him at the warmth that radiated from the boy's skin.

At least he was alive. Feverish, but he could recover from that.

"Matisse, can you hear me?" He patted the boy's cheek hard enough to get the blood flowing. He couldn't tell whether the lad's eyes were open or not. He'd have to rely on an answer.

A groan was his only response, but it was enough. Matisse was conscious, at least somewhat.

Samuel straightened and forced his mind to focus on what should be done first. The fire. They needed warmth and food. Then Moriah and the baby had to rest, and he'd have to see what he could do about Matisse's arm and leg.

His stomach churned at the thought of trying to set the limbs. Could he even do that? He was no doctor, and had only a general idea of what was involved with lining up the bones. How would he know if he had the broken pieces straight? He could barely see more than outlines and shapes, and in addition to his eyes leaking like a mountain river in spring thaw, they ached as though he'd been punched in both sockets.

Was this part of the same sickness Moriah and the baby had? She'd not complained of problems with her eyes. But his own ailments were the least of their concerns. He had to get the fire going. Then food.

Then they needed help.

~

*M*oriah could barely hold back the trembling in her bones as she slipped from her horse. She would have gone down to her knees had she not been clutching the saddle. The cold had gripped her in its icy vice, and she couldn't seem to stop the shakes racking her body. But she had to get to Matisse and see how she could help.

Leaving her horse beside Samuel's, she forced her feet to carry her toward the voices. Matisse lay sprawled on the ground, and Samuel was kneeling over the remnants of what must have been the fire.

She dropped to her knees beside the boy and removed her gloves. One touch of his face heated her hands better than the gloves had. "He's burning up. Where else is he hurt?"

"Right leg at the thigh, and right upper arm." Samuel didn't turn from his work.

She eased the fur cape she'd given the lad away from his arm and flinched at the horribly swollen sleeve. "I'm so sorry, Matisse. But we're here now. We'll get you feeling better."

After a glimpse of that arm, she didn't need to see the leg to take Samuel's word for the injury. Just now, the boy needed any little bit of relief she could offer him. She cradled his face, relishing the heat emanating from his skin. "Can you hear me, Matisse?"

He hadn't opened his eyes, but his breathing seemed to take effort. Maybe that's where all his energy was going. His lips parted, as though he was going to speak. She leaned close to hear, but no sound came out. Instead, his Adam's apple bobbed as he swallowed.

"Are you thirsty?" He must be, with a fever that high. She shifted toward a patch of unblemished snow and scooped the icy crystals in her hands.

Moving back to the lad, she placed a pinch of the ice between his parted lips. "Here. This will help."

Her hands were stinging from cold by the time she fed him the last of what hadn't melted, but at least he was swallowing it on his own.

She glanced over at Samuel, who still knelt over the cold fire. His broad back concealed what he was doing. "How can I help, Samuel?"

He let out a grunt of frustration. "Do you have more dry tender in your saddle pack? I can't get a spark to light."

"I think so." She stood and tucked her numb hands in her coat as she strode back to her mare. Samuel was usually quick with a fire. It was unlike him to be working at it this long without nurturing a single flame. The tightness in her chest clenched harder. Was he getting sick too?

God, no. Please don't let Samuel be ill. Her rock. The strength she'd come to depend on in this crisis that surrounded them.

Maybe he was only delayed because he still held Cherry, sleeping in her sling. She should have taken the baby from him when she'd first dismounted.

With her fire-making kit in hand, she slipped back to where Samuel was working and knelt beside him at the ashes of the fire. He had bark mounded over a bit of cloth and was striking flint against steel, but the way his hands were positioned, the sparks were completely missing the pile of tender.

"Shall I try for a minute?" His gloves were off, as were hers, so maybe his hands were so cold they weren't acting as he told them to.

He handed over the flint and steel, and as she took them, she glanced up at his face. The sight there caught her short.

He was…crying? Tears streamed down his cheeks, and the whites of his eyes were a bright red, as though he'd been sobbing for an hour.

"Samuel, what's wrong?" She cupped a hand over his cheek, wiping away the moisture with her thumb. But the moment the words were out, she wanted to bite them back. She shouldn't ask such a silly question. *Everything* was wrong. But she'd never imagined she'd see this grown man weep.

Did he expect Matisse to die?

He raised a sleeve to wipe away the tears from the cheek she wasn't touching. "My eyes. I don't know why they won't stop this. Makes it hard to see straight." His voice didn't sound hoarse or rough like he'd been crying.

Still, she did her best to catch his gaze. "He'll make it, Samuel. I'm sure he will. We'll all make it through this."

He was looking at her, but his gaze didn't hold the normal intensity she loved about him. In fact, he didn't seem to be focusing on anything in particular.

"I know we will." He closed his hand over hers, which still rested on his cheek. "We have to get this fire going."

She nodded and pulled away, turning back to the tent of bark. After adding a few pieces from her bundle, she struck the flint, and within a minute or two, she'd nurtured a tiny flame. "Is there dry wood to add?"

"I think there's a little left here." He reached for the remnants of a pine branch. His hand missed it completely at first, and he fumbled over the ground until his fingers brushed the limb.

Fear clutched tighter in her chest. Could he not see through his tears?

She glanced at his face again. Those eyes were so bloodshot, they almost looked frightening in the dim light of early dawn.

Then a memory crept in. Something she wasn't even sure was real, just a dim picture from her earliest recollections. Red Hawk, the man her mother had married after she was born, sitting in their lodge, his eyes as red as Samuel's were now. Tears streamed down his face, and he'd sat quietly by the fire. When her mother brought him food, he'd fumbled for it the same way Samuel had for the log.

The sight of the big strong warrior forced to sit, dependent on others to bring him what he needed, to lead him where he had to go, had frightened her as a young girl.

It frightened her now.

"Samuel." She gripped his arm.

He turned to her, pulling the branch with him. "Yes?"

She studied his reddened eyes. He definitely wasn't focusing on her. "Can you see me?"

Tears continued to leak down his face, and he turned away from her. "I'm fine. We need to get this fire going and the meat cooking."

He wasn't fine. But maybe he was right. They had to get warmth and food. Then she could worry about Samuel's and Matisse's injuries.

A half hour later, it turned out she had more to do before she could tend to wounds. Cherry had awakened, crying frantically—probably from hunger, for nursing was the only thing that would silence her tears.

Samuel unsaddled the horses and brought the meat to roast over the growing flame. She hated leaving him to attempt the work alone, but he seemed to manage by keeping a free hand to feel along his way.

Her heart ached at the sight of his struggles, but there was nothing she could do until Cherry was fed.

The babe finally slipped back to sleep, and Moriah positioned her in a bundle of blankets close enough to the fire that she could feel its warmth.

As Samuel dropped to his knees with the bundle of meat, Moriah stood. "I'll get a stick for roasting." They'd need a great deal more wood, too, to keep the fire going.

By the time the meat was almost ready, she had a pot of snow melted so they could all drink and had even coaxed a half cupful into Matisse. "Are you ready to eat now?" She brushed the sweat-dampened hair from his hot forehead. Maybe she should pack snow to cool him, but that seemed just short of torturous in this weather.

He groaned, and his eyes slipped open for the first time. "Hurts."

"I know." She ached for what he must be enduring. If there was a way she could take some of the pain on herself, she would. "Eating will give you strength."

"Moriah." Samuel's voice pulled her focus from the lad.

Something about his tone sounded a warning within her. What now?

CHAPTER 21

"This helplessness... Lord, please."
~ Samuel

*M*oriah walked to the fire, taking a place where she could see Samuel's face. He looked to the flames, but his gaze remained unfocused.

"What is it, Samuel?" She reached for his hand, needing the strength of his touch more than she wanted to admit.

He took her hand, weaving his fingers through hers. Holding her securely. "My family's valley is less than a day's ride from here. Before I found Matisse, I recognized that butte out there with the boulder on top." He motioned in the distance, through the trees. In the dim light of dawn, she saw what he meant. An interesting landmark. Recognizable, to be sure.

"I'm going to ride for help. My brother can come back with a sleigh to move Matisse. I think the break in his arm may have pierced the skin, and there's no way I can set that out here. He needs someone who knows what they're doing." His words loosed a torrent of conflicting emotions in her chest.

Help. They needed it so desperately.

The thought of others—capable and prepared to step in and accomplish what she couldn't—filled her with more relief than she should allow.

But Samuel couldn't ride in his condition. How could he see the path he should take?

She squeezed his hand, determination building inside her. "I'll go. Can you tell me how to find your people?" *And, Lord, don't let them have disappeared like my own did.*

He shook his head, his jaw locking like a vise. "I'll not send you out in the wilderness on your own. I'll leave as soon as I eat."

She reached for his cheek and turned his head to face her. "Look at me, Samuel. Tell me, are my eyes open or closed?" She closed only her right eye, but made sure the left was wide open. This would give her a better idea how deteriorated his vision had become.

He looked at her, but again his eyes didn't seem to focus on any single point. He blinked, tears still leaking down his cheeks, but not as much as before.

"They're...closed." He spoke with certainty, although maybe he was adding bluster to make her think he was well.

Her fear blew out in a frustrated breath. "Only my right eye was closed." She reached for his other hand. "I think something like this happened to my mother's husband when I was little. I don't remember much about it, but he had the same bright red eyes that cried without his control, and he couldn't see for a time. He recovered, though." She gripped his hands, willing him to understand. "You'll recover, too, but we can't wait for that. I need to ride for help."

"Moriah." His voice held an edge of anger. Or maybe fear. "I'm not letting you go."

"Someone needs to stay with Matisse. We can't leave him here to freeze. He needs to be kept warm and made to eat and drink." She glanced at the meat roasting. "The food's ready now."

As she released his hands and reached to divvy portions for each of them, he let out a grunt of frustration. "What of Cherry?"

"She'll go with me. She'll need to nurse." The more she thought about it, the more this path felt right. She'd eat, gather enough firewood to last Samuel a full day and night, have him tell her the route, then ready her horse and leave.

Every minute mattered.

~

Samuel had never felt so helpless.

Moriah was right about him being half-blind. Maybe closer to full-blind. And that was the only reason he hadn't already leapt on his horse and struck out to get help. But letting her and Cherry ride away into the snowy wilderness carrying barely enough food to last a day... How could he allow it? How could he stand it?

He gritted his teeth and pushed to his feet. She was gathering firewood, but the least he could do was ready the horse. He stood still for a moment to try to bring his vision into focus. What in the wild west had he done to make this happen? Was it an effect of the cold? Or maybe from that blinding sun when he'd been looking for Matisse the day before?

Only shadows and vague forms showed before him. He blinked, then tried to focus again. His head went light, and he threw his arms out to balance himself. Was Cherry still lying on the ground next to him? He couldn't fall on top of her.

He stepped away from where she'd been the last time he saw her, then reached for a tree or something else he could use as a guide. What a useless bunch of bones he was. Could Moriah see him blundering through these few simple steps?

Maybe it was best she and the baby leave. For her to see him so helpless like this was humiliating. *She* was strong and brave and capable. Hadn't she proved that by how long she'd lived with only herself and a newborn? She'd even given birth by herself—it was almost unfathomable.

Footsteps sounded behind him, a soft padding in the snow, then the clunk of branches settling against each other.

"That's all the dry wood I could find," she said, "but I think it'll be enough to get you through to tomorrow morning. I should be back with help by then. And maybe your eyes will have healed some." Her voice drew closer as she spoke, then her hand slipped into his.

He gripped her, clinging to the feel of her. Would this be the last time? *God, no.*

"Moriah." His voice rasped with the fear he struggled to hold down. "We need to pray."

He released the tree and reached for her other hand, and she took his willingly. Holding her close, he raised his petitions to God— placing her and Cherry in the hands of the only One who had true control of their journey.

And if the burn in his throat was any indication, these tears still slipping from his eyes might now be real.

~

*M*oriah ducked against the onslaught of blowing snow later that afternoon as she pushed the gelding onward through the white curtain pelting them. Samuel had insisted she ride his gelding, even though the horse had already traveled a great deal in the past night and day. Taking her mare would require allowing the yearling to tag along, and the less she had to worry about the better.

Even as tired as the horse was, she could still feel his unleashed power. Just as magnificent as his owner.

Cherry squirmed in the sling, more than weary of being so confined. And still feverish the last time Moriah checked her. Would they ever find a safe haven where they could all heal? The thought of a peaceful valley with a warm cabin, plenty of food, and people willing to help—people she didn't have to fear—seemed like a dream that could never truly happen.

Maybe Samuel's people were accepting of him, but would they open their doors to an Indian? Or worse, a mixed-blood? She wanted to curse the foul cur who'd fathered her, but she forced herself to cling to the prayer Samuel had prayed before she mounted the horse.

This God she wanted so badly to trust...would He see her to safety? *Please.* It was the only prayer her exhausted heart could summon.

She forced herself to raise her face into the blowing snow. She had to watch for the mountain on her left with the ring of trees circling its base. That could describe half the mountains in this territory, but so far, each of the landmarks Samuel had given her showed exactly as he said they would.

Another half hour later, the snow still fell, but at least the wind wasn't blowing as hard. The mountain she was watching for still hadn't presented itself. She'd seen two other peaks, both with patches of scrawny trees scattered over their bases and sides, but not one with trees spanning in an unbroken ring around the base.

Had he said how far she'd need to travel to reach that mountain? He'd only given two more landmarks after that one, so surely she'd be close at that point.

Tension balled the knot tighter in her belly, whether from the thought of being lost or the thought of meeting strangers, she couldn't have said.

Another hour passed, with no sign of the mountain. She'd had to stop and position Cherry for nursing, but then she'd pressed on, letting the babe eat and fall back to sleep as they rode. The roasted meat she'd brought for herself was long gone, and darkness was closing around them like a death shroud.

The falling snow was finally dying away, but the icy wind wouldn't relent. The oppressive clouds blocked out any moon or stars, so the brightness of the snow was her only light. Would she be able to see the mountains in the darkness? Maybe she'd veered too far to the left to find the landmarks Samuel gave her.

God, help me. Please.

Time seemed to crawl by, and she couldn't tell whether they'd been riding for minutes or hours. She must have missed the mountain.

Should she turn back? Or turn to the right as she was supposed to do when she passed that landmark?

Samuel and Matisse needed her to bring help. She'd only left them enough wood to last until morning. If she found Samuel's brother in the next hour and he was able to leave with her immediately, they'd be hard-pressed to reach Samuel and Matisse by the time their fire died.

Lord, let Samuel's sight be better. He would be able to care for them both if he could only see. At least they had the rest of the meat he could cook as they needed it.

She reined the gelding to the right, mostly because continuing straight seemed futile when she'd surely passed the landmark without seeing it in the dark. And turning back seemed unthinkable, when every step to reach this far had been torturous.

A stretch of trees spanned along her left side, and she kept the horse moving beside them. Could these be the trees that circled the base of the mountain she'd been looking for? If so, the instructions called for her to ride past them before turning. But she still couldn't see a peak rising up behind the tall pines.

Lord, show me. Guide us to the right place.

As they rode, a mountain rose up on her right, and the farther they traveled, the tighter the passage between the cliff and the trees narrowed. She'd be forced to ride into the woods soon.

Or maybe she should turn around? *Oh, God. What do I do?*

Cherry was squirming again in the sling, but she hadn't started fussing yet. Moriah used her free hand to cradle the babe's body. Maybe her touch would help soothe.

A thin strip of ground ran between the trees and the cliff, and she kept the gelding there. Could this be a path? Maybe a game trail. It seemed too much to hope that this stretch of ground might be ridden regularly by humans.

By Samuel's family.

Without a wide stretch of white snow, the darkness closed in tighter and tighter. Maybe she should turn around.

A horse and rider appeared in front of her, about twenty strides ahead. Her heart surged into her throat, and she pulled the gelding to a stop.

Could this be one of Samuel's family? If so, that must be God's doing.

But it could be anyone. A trapper. An Indian.

She rested her hand on the butt of her rifle. Should she pull it onto her lap so she'd be ready to fire, or wait and try to keep the exchange friendly?

The stranger rode toward her, and she forced herself to sit stoically in the saddle. Not to cradle Cherry's sling, which would alert the new arrival to her vulnerable child.

The man approaching wore a fur hood, and the shadows made it impossible to see his face. But as he neared, the glimmer of a rifle barrel showed all too clear.

And it was pointed right at her.

CHAPTER 22

"Help doesn't look at all as I imagined it...or maybe it does."
~ Moriah

*M*oriah closed her hand around her own gun and eased it upward, working the barrel out of the scabbard.

"Leave that rifle right where it's at." The voice dripped with deadly menace, but in a much higher pitch than she'd expected. Was this a woman?

Confidence flared inside her. She could face off with any female who came against her, even with a rifle aimed her way. Still, she stopped moving, holding the gun halfway out of its holder.

"Who are you? What's your business here?" Definitely a woman, although she had the art of gruffness well-mastered. She reined in about two horse-lengths away.

Should Moriah tell her full story or hold back? If this was one of Samuel's family, the stranger would need details before she would drop her guard.

She forced her voice to carry strength. "I am Moriah Clark. I've been traveling with Samuel Grant, but he's injured and sent me ahead to find his family. Do you know the Grant family who live in a valley near here?"

Shadows still masked the woman's face, but Moriah kept her gaze on the rifle. If this stranger knew Samuel's family, she would lower the gun and greet her. Or at least be civil.

If anything, the grip on the rifle tightened.

Moriah held her tongue. Let this stranger explain herself now.

"How do you know Samuel Grant?"

Hope burgeoned inside her for the first time in hours. This woman must know him. Maybe she was part of his family and simply being protective.

"He came to find my husband, then offered to take me to my people in the mountains. When we couldn't find them, we turned south to seek shelter with Samuel's family." She was so accustomed to keeping Henry's death secret, she'd not mentioned it in her explanation. But that was a good thing. She'd hate for word of his passing to be shared callously with his sister.

"Who else is traveling with you?"

"I am alone right now." Except for the baby, but she wouldn't announce her presence yet. "A lad has been riding with us, but he's badly injured. He and Samuel wait for me to bring back help."

"Come with me then." The woman lowered the gun and reined her horse to the side so Moriah could pass. She didn't put the rifle away though, just rested it across her lap.

She obeyed, nudging the gelding forward. As she rode past the other woman, she tried to get a glance at her face, but saw nothing more than a pale cheek not hidden by the shadows.

Lord, let her be taking me to Rachel. Surely Henry's sister would help her, even if Samuel's people proved to be just as she feared—untrustworthy and unwilling to let a strange half-Indian into their midst.

"Turn on that trail into the woods." The woman's bark came just as they reached the place where she'd appeared a few minutes before. This must be the path back to her dwelling.

They rode through darkness, a night so black she could barely see the forms of trees around her. She had to trust the gelding to stay on the path and assume that the woman riding behind her would comment if they strayed too far in the wrong direction.

At last, they emerged from the trees. A hill rose just ahead of them. Not a mountain, but at least as tall as the cabin Henry had built her.

"Follow those tracks up and over."

Moriah obeyed, aiming the gelding toward what looked to be a well-trodden path through the snow.

As they crested the top, a cabin appeared. Light shone through a glass window. *Real* glass. Something she'd only seen at the fort.

"Turn to the right toward that cabin in the distance."

Moriah looked that direction, finally spotting another bit of light. This one outlined the shape of another building, with the light coming from the opposite side of the structure.

As she turned the gelding that way, Cherry began squirming again and let out a complaining whimper. Moriah rested her hand under the baby, patting to hopefully soothe her. This may be the valley Samuel spoke of, but until she determined whether the people meant her harm or help, her daughter would be much safer if they didn't know about her. She'd seen and heard of horrible things done to women and children—the more helpless, the worse the treatment.

And she wouldn't let *any* of that happen to Cherry.

They neared the cabin where the woman had directed, and Moriah rode around the building toward the light where the door must be. The glow was coming through a window—again, covered with real glass—and was bright enough to show another building across the yard. That one might be a barn, but it was hard to tell at night.

"Stop by the stairs." The woman motioned toward the steps leading up onto the porch.

As Moriah complied, her captor raised her voice and called loud enough for those inside to hear. "Seth!"

Hadn't Samuel said his brother's name was Seth? The brother who would be marrying Rachel?

A scuffling noise inside preceded the opening of the door. A man stepped forward, lantern in one hand and rifle in the other, with shoulders wide enough to almost fill the frame.

Samuel. Her heart stuttered even as her mind told her this man couldn't be him. The broad shoulders, every part of his outline was so similar. Could this be Samuel's twin, Seth?

"Rachel?" He stepped onto the porch, raising the light as he studied them both. "Who is this? What's wrong?"

"I found her riding alone on the other side of the trees beyond this hill." The woman's voice wasn't nearly as terse when she spoke to Seth, but she still kept a no-nonsense tone. "She said she's been traveling with Samuel and a boy, but she hasn't said anything about my brother."

My brother. This was Rachel? She didn't seem at all like the loving big sister Henry had described. Maybe sharing more details would help these two realize who she was and that she was only here seeking help.

Moriah turned to face her. "Are you Rachel?" With the light from the lantern, she could finally see the woman's face—and the way her pretty brows rose at the question.

"How do you know my name?" The question wasn't tinged with challenge, as she would have expected, but simple curiosity.

"My husband, Henry—your brother—told me much about you. He read me your letters. We didn't know you were planning to come to our land." She softened her voice. "He would have loved to see you again, but he died over six months ago."

The woman's face shifted, losing its serious glare. The rifle in her hand wavered, then she seemed to tighten her grip. "How do you know that? And how can you be his wife? Henry never married."

A stab pierced her chest. Hadn't he told his sister about her? He'd written at least two letters to Rachel after they married. Why would he keep her a secret?

Unless he was ashamed... The thought pressed down on her like an avalanche.

He'd never seemed embarrassed of her in the fort. Had always championed her when the men grew rude and offensive. But maybe he'd not been able to bring himself to admit to his family that he'd married a Peigan woman. A half-blood.

Tears stung her eyes, but she forced them back. Forced her shoulders to square and her chin to stay steady. "Henry and I have been married for two years. We have a child—a girl. I'm sorry if he was ashamed to tell you of me."

The woman stared at her another minute, and even with the light from the lantern, Moriah couldn't decipher any emotions that crossed her face. Perhaps shock, but she wasn't certain.

Then with deliberate movements, she lowered the rifle, replaced the gun into its scabbard, and dismounted. Leaving her horse, she strode forward and stopped by Moriah, placing her hand on the gelding's shoulder.

When she looked up, shadows hid half her face, but the visible eye was clearly focused on Moriah. "What did you say your name was?"

"Moriah Clark."

"Your daughter...where is she?"

Moriah hesitated. Did she dare reveal the babe? Even as she pondered, Cherry gave a sharp squirm in the sling. Moriah pushed aside the buffalo robe covering her to reveal the little bundle. "She is here."

A sharp intake of breath jerked Moriah's focus back to the woman —to Rachel. "Come inside. Please. You both need to get out of this cold."

Some of the tension eased out of her, but now the real work had come. "I can't. Samuel and Matisse need help. They're at the base of a mountain about a day's ride from here. Matisse has bad breaks in his leg and arm and a high fever. Something happened to Samuel's eyes and he can't see. They have enough firewood and meat to last until morning, but they need help soon. Do you have a sleigh or wagon we can take to get them? Matisse is in a bad way." Once she started, the words seemed to gush out of her. Had she said everything important? "They need blankets. And food."

A movement on the porch pulled her attention from Rachel. Seth had turned away and was calling inside. "Simeon, Emma. We need help."

Rachel touched her leg, drawing her gaze back down. "We'll go get them, don't worry. I'm sure Simeon can find them if you give directions. And he's the best doctor around. Come inside and get warm. You must be hungry too."

A new wave of relief seeped through her, stealing the strength from her shoulders. "Thank you. I'll ride back with them. Do you think I can ride in the wagon? This gelding hasn't had much rest in the last two days."

"Climb down and we'll talk inside. You have to warm yourself."

Rachel was probably right. A few minutes by a fire would do her a world of good. And she needed to pull Cherry out of the sling and change her quickly before they set out.

After grabbing what she'd need from her pack, she dismounted and allowed Rachel to guide her up onto the porch.

Seth passed them on his way out, brushing Rachel's arm as he passed. His face was similar to Samuel's but not identical. He spoke in a low voice, clearly meant for Rachel. "Simeon's gathering supplies. I'm going to harness the team. Can Emma use your horse to ride over and tell Noelle?"

"Of course." The look that passed between them held more than Moriah was able to unpack. Angst, yes, but also a kind of mutual comfort, as though they drew strength from each other.

Her heart squeezed at the thought, calling forth all her memories of Samuel. She felt that way every time he was near.

They had to bring him and Matisse to safety. Anything could happen to them out there, and if she lost Samuel, she wasn't sure she could carry on. He'd taken over her heart in a way she might never recover from.

She turned and started through the door. Rachel stepped inside behind her as Moriah let her eyes adjust to the light and take in the scene. A homey room with a large fireplace on the wall to the left. To the right, a man stood working over the table that dominated the area, and against the wall stood a cookstove. She'd only seen one of those in her life and had to force herself not to gawk now.

"Come sit by the fire." Rachel tapped her arm, and the words shifted Moriah into motion. "What do you need for the baby? I'll get you food."

She pulled Cherry from the sling as she moved toward the blazing fire in the hearth. "I just need to change her. Here on the floor is fine."

Rachel left her alone to tend the little one, which was a relief, for Cherry's patience had worn away. She cried as Moriah wrapped her in a clean cloth, forcing a plump fist into her mouth to show how hungry she was. She'd have to nurse as they rode in the wagon. Hopefully the men would allow her to ride in the back with the supplies.

When the babe was bundled again in clean blankets, Moriah raised her daughter to her shoulder and rubbed her back to soothe her. Cherry's favorite position helped, and her cries faded to murmurs.

Rachel approached with a bowl. "Here's stew. Would you like to tend her in one of the bedchambers? It won't be as warm there, but you'd have privacy."

The aroma drifting from that stew was impossible to ignore, especially when her midsection churned in a noisy growl. Her head seemed to lighten as if just the sight of food stole away some of her strength.

"Here. Sit in this chair and eat by the fire." Rachel placed the bowl on a table beside a large fabric-covered chair. "Let me hold the baby. My...niece." She stumbled on the word, and when she turned back to Moriah, her eyes held a glimmer of emotion.

Should she allow her to take Cherry? She did want Henry's sister to know his daughter. And she'd do better on the trip ahead if she had warm food inside her. Cherry could nurse along the way.

Easing the babe from her chest and into Rachel's arms took more strength of will than she'd prepared herself for. She had to swallow down the tears that threatened her own eyes. "You'll want to keep her close to me. So she doesn't cry." Although the request was really more for her own peace than the babe's.

Rachel positioned Cherry against her chest the way Moriah had, bouncing and talking sweetly as she rubbed circles in her back.

Moriah forced herself to sit and take up the bowl, but every one of her muscles tensed to spring forward should she need to reach her daughter. She gulped the stew, and when the bowl was empty, she couldn't have said what she ate.

Rachel turned to her with a smile so soft it was almost angelic. An effect of holding Cherry, no doubt. "She's lovely, Moriah. Do you mind if I call you, Moriah? I'm still trying to wrap my mind around my little brother being married, with a daughter." Her expression changed, and red rimmed her eyes. "How long did you say he's been gone?"

"Almost seven months." Although it seemed so much longer now. These last weeks had felt like a different lifetime than her days alone in the cabin.

The shimmer in Rachel's eyes thickened. "So he never knew his daughter. Did he know she was coming?"

Moriah swallowed down the emotion that threatened to clog her throat. "He was very excited about the baby."

Rachel turned away. Moriah couldn't blame her for trying to hide her emotion. Cherry started to fuss again, and she moved back to hand over the babe.

Having her daughter in her arms again soothed a balm over her frayed nerves, and she inhaled the sweet baby scent.

But she couldn't linger there long. Samuel and Matisse needed her.

CHAPTER 23

"I can't rest yet."
~ Samuel

*M*oriah glanced back toward the table where the man had been standing, but he was gone now. "Do you think they're ready?" Maybe she should go out and help them prepare.

"Moriah." Rachel stepped closer. "You're exhausted. Simeon and Seth will bring back Samuel and the boy. I suspect Noelle, their sister, and her husband will go too. Please stay here. For your baby. There's nothing more you could do that they aren't able to."

Moriah tried to back away, but her legs hit the chair, stilling her. But it didn't stop the turmoil spinning in her chest. "I told Samuel I would be back. He needs me. I can't leave him out there." *Oh, God.* Just the thought of entrusting Samuel to the mercy of others clutched her chest with fear.

"Moriah." Thankfully, Rachel didn't step closer again, but her voice dropped to a soothing tone. "They love him, too. They're his family.

They'll make sure they bring him back. And you'll be rested and ready to help him when he gets here."

Her throat tightened, and she forced herself to draw in slow, steady breaths, just like she'd done the night she gave birth to Cherry.

Rachel was right. These were Samuel's people, and they would surely do their best to bring him and Matisse back. But if something happened and he didn't return alive, she would never forgive herself. What if they couldn't find the landmark? They might wander for hours, or even days—precious time that might determine life or death for Samuel and Matisse.

"I'll bring Simeon in so you can tell him exactly where they are. He's lived out here at least a dozen years, so he knows every landmark around."

Moriah summoned a nod, although it surely looked weak. She would tell this Simeon the directions, then decide whether he was capable of bringing back her men in time.

Less than a minute later, the cabin door opened, and a man stepped inside. The same one who'd been standing by the table earlier, although now he was bundled tightly in a furskin coat. He turned and strode toward them with long intentional strides. The closer he came, the larger he loomed, both from sheer height and the span of his shoulders.

She held her chin high.

He nodded a greeting. "I'm Simeon Grant, and you must be Mrs. Clark. Glad you found us. Can you tell me exactly where Samuel and the boy are?"

She described the unusual butte with the boulder on top, and he nodded immediately like he knew well the landmark. And when she told of the trees where they were camped, he nodded again.

"We'll push hard and try to get there by first light. You said the boy has broken limbs and a fever? What's wrong with my brother?"

"His eyes are bright red and streaming tears, and he's able to see very little. It started a few hours before I left, and seemed to get worse quickly."

Simeon's brow furrowed. "Maybe the bright sun damaged his eyes.

We'll see what we can do about it. We're leaving now. Keep praying for them both until we get back." He turned to Rachel. "Daniel and Noelle are riding with us. Can you go over to their cabin and bring their young'uns and your son over when they wake up?"

She nodded, then the man turned and strode toward the door. Within seconds, even the sound of his boots on the porch was gone.

Moriah stared toward the place where he'd disappeared, every part of her longing to sprint after him. The only thing that held her in place were the words Simeon had said. *Keep praying.*

Samuel's prayer from before she left soaked back through her, wrapping her in the feeling she'd had while he spoke the words. He hadn't just been talking into the wind. He'd been earnestly entreating a God he *knew*. As though he trusted that God would really answer those prayers.

And God had brought her here, to Samuel's people. They were on their way, even now, to help him and Matisse.

She sank down into the chair, clutching Cherry to her. Squeezing her eyes shut as she lifted her heart to God. *I want to know you like that, God. I want to have that kind of faith. Show me how.*

~

Samuel sat by Matisse, holding a cup of meat broth to his lips as the lad sipped. He'd cast up the roasted meat they'd tried earlier, so Samuel was attempting warm broth this time. The boy needed some kind of nutrients, both because he'd gone so long without food and because his body would require all the strength they could give it.

Matisse sank back, and Samuel pulled the cup away. Moisture still dampened his brow, and he lay now with his eyes closed, breathing hard. The pain had to be excruciating, but Matisse never complained aloud. Only occasional moans, but otherwise, tortured silence.

He raised his gaze to where Moriah had ridden into the distance the day before. A full day, now that the blush of sunrise had faded into gray winter sky. At least he could see the sky now. Thank the Lord his eyesight had mostly recovered. His eyes still burned and his vision blurred a little, but tears no longer leaked uncontrollably.

They could make it a little longer until Moriah came back. If she didn't come in another few hours, he'd have to leave Matisse and hunt today, for he'd used the last of the goat's meat for this broth. The mare and yearling were growing leaner by the day without enough grazing.

But Matisse.

His fever hadn't waned at all, and his injured limbs looked like they would burst the seams of his clothing any moment. How much longer could his body manage under such trauma before it shut down?

A motion in the distance caught his attention, even as a moan from Matisse vied for his focus. What was that? A horse?

He squinted and peered through the trees. *A horse and wagon.* Or something large like that. His vision blurred more the harder he strained.

"Hang in there, son." He swallowed down the knot clogging his throat. "Help is here." He pushed to his feet and stumbled as he tried to step over Matisse. He caught himself on a tree but didn't stop to regain his balance, just lurched forward as fast as his unsteady legs would carry him.

He made it out of the trees and waved both hands. "Here! Help!" He didn't care a whit how ridiculous he looked.

His foot caught on a drift of ice-covered snow, and he tumbled forward. Cold stung his face, seeping down under his coat in a glacial creep that made his whole body go numb.

Voices called in the distance, but with the crunch of snow around him, he couldn't make out words. His entire body ached as he pushed himself upright. His leather gloves hadn't been able to keep the icy dampness from penetrating. For that matter, his pants hadn't either.

When he made it up to his hands and knees, he searched for the wagon again. Closer now. They'd turned toward him, and he could make out two blurry horses along with several figures riding on the seat.

By the time he'd heaved his weary bones to standing, the rig was near enough for him to make out three figures on the wagon seat—Simeon, Noelle, and her husband, Daniel. A minute later, a fourth person jumped from the bed of the moving conveyance and ran toward him.

Seth. He'd never been so happy to see his twin in all his days.

Seth reached him and grabbed hold of his arms. "You're alive." He didn't pull him into a hug, just stood, taking him in from head to toe. "You look like you've spent the last ten years wandering the mountain wilderness…half-starved. But praise God you're alive."

Samuel tried to summon a smile, but he couldn't quite manage it. Instead, he turned and used the last of his strength to motion his brother into the woods. "I hope you brought a blanket for us to move Matisse. He's in a bad way."

~

*H*ours later—he couldn't have said how many—Samuel finally gave in to the gentle swish of the sleigh runners on snow and laid back against the pile of blankets, letting his eyes drift shut. Finally having his belly full of Noelle's sourdough bread and sliced ham and the warmth of being wrapped in layers of blankets seemed too wonderful.

Daniel had stayed behind to pack up their camp and bring the mare and yearling back at a slower pace. Now Simeon was pushing the team that pulled the sleigh hard, for which Samuel was thankful. Matisse lay next to him in the wagon, his labored breathing making it impossible to completely relax.

Noelle sat on the boy's other side, giving him sips of a willow tea to help with the pain. There wasn't much any of them could do until they made it back to Simeon's house. And even then, the setting of those limbs would be excruciating before the agony finally eased. *Lord, could You do him a kindness and let him pass out before the real work begins?*

As evening closed in around them, he forced his eyes open again. His weary bones would sleep if he gave them a chance, but he wanted to be awake when they arrived. He needed to know Moriah was well.

Noelle said she hadn't met her yet, but Seth told an awful story of Rachel finding Moriah wandering in the woods and bringing her to the cabin at gunpoint.

Just the thought of the fear she must have endured tightened the coil in his gut. He well knew the feeling of being held at the point of Rachel's rifle—back when he and Seth first met her—and Moriah certainly hadn't needed the added fear when their situation was already so tenuous.

Finally, they rolled into the valley he'd left weeks before. Noelle and Daniel's cabin was the nearest, but Simeon drove past it to his own, pulling the team just beyond his porch stairs so they could easily carry Matisse up.

Noelle stroked a hand across the lad's brow. "We're finally here, Matisse. We'll get you fixed up in just a few minutes." As bossy a big sister as she'd been, those qualities now made her an excellent nurse. He'd never been so thankful for her.

The cabin door opened, spilling both light and people onto the darkened porch. Many of the figures were small with clamoring voices, but two women separated from the rest, hurrying down the stairs. It wasn't hard to determine which was Moriah, even when all he could see was the shadowed outline of her.

She was the one who made his heart beat faster. The one whose presence drew him from the wagon bed as the others moved in to care for Matisse. She met him the moment his feet touched the ground, stepping into him with open arms. "Samuel."

He wrapped himself around her, breathing her in, holding on with every bit of strength he had left. Letting his embrace tell her everything he couldn't find the words to say.

She clung to him at first, but then eased back. He wanted to pull her close again, but he also needed to get her in out of the cold.

She didn't pull completely from his arms, though. Just enough so she could study his face. "How are you?" Light shining through the windows glimmered in her dark eyes, showing him the worry there.

He slipped his hands up to cradle her face and lowered his mouth to press a kiss to her lips. A better way to answer her question than any words he might have used. He'd meant it as only a gentle brushing, but the hunger in her response almost drew him in for more. Still, with his family scurrying about, this wasn't the place.

Pulling back, he let his eyes roam her face, drinking their fill of her beauty. "I'm fine. What about you? And Cherry?"

"Much better. Your sister gave her something that finally broke the fever, and she's sleeping." She reached up to touch his temple. "Your eyes? Can you see now?"

He nodded. "Almost back to normal. Just a little blurry at times."

The sheen in her own gaze thickened. "Samuel." Her voice cracked on his name. As much as he wanted her to let down her guard, this wasn't the place. Not in the cold with so much chaos around them.

He pressed his fingers to her lips. "Let's go in."

CHAPTER 24

"This gift...I never knew how much I wanted it."
~ Moriah

*L*ess than an hour later, Moriah squeezed her hands against her ears to close out the feral scream radiating through the house. Her entire body ached with the pain Matisse must be enduring as they set his broken bones. *God, give him strength.*

Suddenly, the cry ceased in the midst of a breath.

She eased out her own pent-up air, pulling her hands away to hear what was happening in the next room.

"Easy there, Little Bit. He's going to be all better soon." Samuel stood by the hearth, swaying and bouncing Cherry as she fussed. Moriah couldn't blame her daughter a bit. Matisse's cries had been heart-wrenching.

She met Samuel's eyes. "Do you think he passed out?"

"I hope so. I'm glad Seth and Rachel took the children out to the barn." His gaze held warm concern and the same earnestness she always loved about his expression. This man may seem quiet and reserved, but he lived with an intensity that was slowly bringing her back to life.

She couldn't help the love that swelled in her chest. It didn't seem love could be possible after only these few weeks together, but with the depth of what they'd been through, she felt as though she knew Samuel—the real man inside him—better than she'd known Henry after a year of marriage.

Her gaze slipped to her daughter, who lay against Samuel's shoulder with eyes wide open and a fist in her mouth. Even Cherry drew strength and pleasure from just being near him.

Moriah walked over to the pair, resting her hand on her daughter's back but letting her gaze roam Samuel's face. "You must be exhausted. Lay down and rest now. I'll make a pallet by the fire."

"I'll sleep when I know Matisse is settled. I got a little rest last night, so I'm not bad off."

She could tell by the weary lines and shadows around his eyes that he was exhausted, but if his midsection churned the way hers did, he wouldn't be able to relax until they knew everything possible had been done for the boy.

A quarter hour later, she'd taken the baby and finally coaxed Samuel into resting in the big chair nearest the fire when the door to one of the bedchambers opened. Out stepped a weary Simeon Grant, Daniel following.

Simeon's sleeves were rolled, showing his massive forearms, but it was his face she studied longest. Daniel stepped past the taller man and strode toward the door, a pot in his hand.

"How is he?" Samuel rose to his feet, moving toward his oldest brother.

Simeon eased out a haggard breath. "Both were bad. I think the leg is a clean break, but that area swelled an awful lot. The arm bone had punctured the skin, and with the swelling there, it wasn't easy setting the break. We'll have to watch that one closely."

"You think he'll mend completely?"

Simeon placed a wad of bandages on the table. "If that arm doesn't get infected, he should live. He may have a limp, and I'm not sure how straight the arm will be. If we can get the swelling down in the next day or two, I'll be able to check the set of the bone."

He should live. There was still a chance they might lose him? Not Matisse, who'd been a blessing every step of their journey. *Lord, please make him live.* "Is he awake?"

Simeon shook his head. "Not really. He lost consciousness when we set the arm. He's just mumbling now. Emma and Noelle are both with him, and Daniel went to get snow to pack around the swelling. We've done everything we can right now. The girls will take turns with him through the night."

"I'll help." She started forward, but Samuel snagged her arm.

"Why don't you let them handle it just for tonight? You need rest. My sister lives to nurse people, so Matisse is in good hands."

Simeon nodded. "He's right. There's another bed in the room he's in, but you'll never get sleep in there. You and the baby take our bed. I think the young'uns will stay at the other house with Rachel."

Moriah wavered. She wasn't about to put this man out of his bed. And it sounded like Rachel might have her hands full. Maybe she should be over there helping.

"Moriah." Samuel's thumb stroked her arm. "Do what Simeon says. Tomorrow we'll start fresh, and there will be plenty to do. For now, everything is taken care of."

Was it? It had been so long since she'd had this many people to share the load. Not since she'd left her family. It was hard to adjust when she wasn't the only one to do what had to be done.

Samuel's hand gently pushed her toward the door to the chamber where Cherry had napped earlier. It had clearly been the room belonging to the master and mistress of the place.

She glanced at Simeon. "I'll just lay some blankets on the floor in here. I don't need a mattress." She'd never had one until after she married Henry.

Samuel's hand shifted on her arm, and his other slipped around her back. "Come in here where Simeon said. This is the best place for you and Little Bit. If you need anything at all, I'll be right out here by the fire."

Simeon turned back toward the other chamber where Matisse lay. "Sleep well. I'll send Emma in to see if you need anything."

At the doorway, Samuel used his elbow to push open the door. "We'll get you some hot stones to warm the bed. I'm sure Emma will bring a lantern. Anything else you need?"

She turned to face him, not quite ready to step into the dark room alone. "My pack is already in here from when I laid Cherry down." The babe gurgled in her arms, as content as she'd been in a long time. Moriah searched his face. "Are you sure this is right?"

Something about the simple act of stepping into the bedchamber felt like a leap of faith. A faith she was still learning to understand.

He leaned forward and pressed a kiss to her forehead. Warm and achingly gentle. Then he drew back to look at her. "You're one of us, too. And we take care of our own." He touched her chin with his fingers, raising her face as he lowered his mouth to hers.

Samuel. Every bit of him strong and sure and just the man she needed.

When he pulled back, all the angst in her chest slipped away, leaving her feeling full and cherished. "Thank you." She wished there was a better way to say what was building inside her.

His mouth quirked up on one side. "For what?"

She pressed a hand to his chest. "For being you." Then she turned and walked into the bedchamber.

～

"There you go. Keep eating like that, and you'll be up and walking soon." Moriah helped Matisse take another sip of water, then replaced the cup on the bedside table. This was the third day since that awful night Simeon had set the broken limbs, and the boy's normal color was finally returning to his ruddy face. "Anything else I can get you?"

He shook his head, then a glimmer of hope touched his tired eyes. "You can get me out of this bed."

She couldn't help reaching up to brush the hair from his brow. His face still had the angles of a growing youth—half-boy, half-man. But he'd proved his strength through the ordeal of the last week. "I'm proud of you, Matisse. I'm so glad God brought our paths together." She had no doubt now that the Heavenly Father had orchestrated the entire trip.

He ducked his chin, lowering his black lashes. "Me, too."

Best she not get too sappy with the boy, but she'd make sure she told him again later. He'd probably grown up feeling abandoned and struggling for every little thing he needed to survive. Yet he'd developed into a special young man, hard-working and good to his core—a son any mother would be proud to call her own.

It was high time someone told him so.

Pushing to her feet, she stepped toward the door. "Just call if you need anything."

As she pulled the door shut behind her, his tired eyes were already drooping. Maybe from the willow tea they'd been pouring into him, or maybe because his body still needed so much energy to heal itself. At least his fever had finally faded.

When she turned and swept her gaze around the main room, her eyes caught on the figure in the rocking chair. Rather, the two figures.

Rachel sat with Cherry lying on her lap. The babe stared up at her aunt with wide eyes while Rachel sang to her. The woman's face radiated with joy, making her even more beautiful than usual.

As the song came to a close, Rachel looked up at Moriah, the sweet smile still softening her face. "I think she likes to be sung to."

Moriah stepped toward them, settling into the armchair beside Rachel. "She seems to like everything you do. Same as with Samuel. She gets excited as soon as she hears his voice."

Rachel turned back to the babe and spoke in animated tones for the little one's pleasure. "From what I've seen, the feeling is mutual." Then she lifted her gaze to Moriah and used her regular voice. "He lights up when he sees this little one. When he sees you, too."

Moriah ducked her head. She wasn't ready to talk about what she felt for Samuel. Especially not with her deceased husband's sister.

Maybe this was the time to say what she'd been wanting to tell

Rachel since she arrived. "Rachel. I'm so sorry about Henry. More sorry than I can say. He was a good man."

The smile slipped from Rachel's face, and she looked at Cherry again, but her mind seemed far away. She was quiet for a while, only the rocking of the chair and an occasional baby coo filling the silence.

At last, she spoke. "I hadn't seen him since I was first married. I still remember him as the sandy-haired little brother I was always trying to keep out of trouble. He was a good boy, though. As much as a little brother can be. I wish I'd seen him once more before he left for the west." Her voice quivered and her eyes glistened. "I wish I'd come to find him sooner."

Moriah's chest ached, knowing well the pain of those wishes. She rested a hand on Rachel's arm. "I'm sorry I was the one who brought Samuel to you and not Henry. If I could give him to you now, I would."

Rachel looked up through the glimmer in her eyes. "I wouldn't trade my new sister and niece for anything." She sniffed, a smile trying to shimmer through her tears. "I've always wanted a sister. Someone who would be my true friend."

A longing rose up in Moriah, choking her throat with emotion. "Me, too." Even with all her siblings, she'd felt like an outsider. Was it possible to find a place she truly belonged? A friend?

Rachel sniffed again. "I should apologize for greeting you at gunpoint. You must have been scared stiff."

At least Moriah could smile about it now. She pulled her hand back to her lap and added a gentle note to her tone. "Samuel told me you have a habit of such welcomes."

The woman looked down, but it didn't hide the color flushing her cheeks. "He told you that, did he? Well, it's a habit I'm trying to break. Or at least be more selective about." She glanced up through her lashes to show a repentant look in her eyes.

"I'm only thankful you didn't shoot me," Moriah said, "and that you brought me here so I could get help. And that the others made it to Samuel and Matisse in time. And that we're all on the mend." Now it was her turn to blush. She could count her blessings for days and not list them all. *Thank You ever so much, Lord.*

Rachel touched Moriah's arm, the contact stilling her. "Moriah, I'm so thankful Samuel found you and brought you here to us. I can see there's something special growing between you, and I just wanted to say I'm glad."

Moriah looked at the woman's hand on her arm, not quite sure she could meet her eyes. How could Rachel say that? Didn't she think Moriah should still be mourning Henry?

And maybe she should be. She'd always remember Henry as a good man and a kind husband. And he was Cherry's father. She would see him in their daughter every time she looked at the babe. But her heart had never known what it felt like to love—truly love—and be offered that same gift in return.

Rachel squeezed her arm. "Love is a special thing. Not something to pass by when you find it."

Moriah did meet her gaze then, and the certainty shimmering there eased the angst in her chest. She nodded. "Thank you…friend."

CHAPTER 25

"One thing yet remains..."
~ Samuel

A week passed before Samuel could catch his breath. Moriah seemed to settle in a little more each day, and the way the women doted on little Cherry, he rarely had a moment alone with the little cherub.

Not that he'd been sitting around pining, since Seth was pushing to get his house finished. He and the other men had spent much of their daylight hours working on the cabin. In another day or two, it'd be ready for furniture.

Then the wedding.

His chest pinched at the thought. He and Seth had been together for everything throughout their entire lives. Now Seth was branching out on his own. Moving in a direction they couldn't travel together, and the loss cut a raw edge somewhere in the vicinity of his heart.

Not that he begrudged his brother. Seth and Rachel were good together. They balanced one another, each making the other better. She'd accomplished something Samuel had never been able to.

But still, he would miss his brother. The one who'd been connected to him since before they were born.

He ambled across the yard outside Simeon's cabin, heading toward the barn. Emma had said Moriah might be out checking her horses. Since this was the Sabbath, Seth had given them a reprieve from building, and he ached to spend it with the woman and child he loved.

Now, if only he could find them.

He pushed open the door enough to slide through, then slowed to let his eyes accustom to the dim lighting. He was still sensitive to changes in lighting, especially harsh sunlight. But thank the Lord his vision had fully returned.

A soft rustling sounded from one of the stalls, and he ambled forward to see if Moriah was the source. She was there, inside the pen with her mare and yearling. The colt stood tied to a wall as she ran a soft brush over his wooly winter coat.

The animal raised his head and nickered as Samuel approached the gate, and Moriah turned to look. A smile settled over her sweet face when she saw him, the kind of smile that warmed him from the inside out.

He leaned on the rail. "Porcupine wounds finally healed?"

She turned back to brush the colt's neck. "Looks like it. I'm trying to spend more time with him so he'll be gentle like his mama." She reached to pat the mare, but a sadness seemed to slip over her face.

He swallowed. "I'm sorry we never found your other mare." Daniel had searched the area before coming back with these two, but the tracks had no longer been visible. Who knew how far the horse had wandered and what it might have fallen prey to.

Her mouth pulled into a smile, but there was no joy in the look. "So am I. But at least we didn't lose Matisse."

Matisse would be a good change of topic. "I just left his room. He said he's feeling good enough to get up and walk around, but you won't allow it."

She rolled her eyes. "He talks big, but he still has a lot of healing to do." She reached for the colt's halter and untied the strap, releasing the horse to walk around the stall. "I guess I'm done here."

He opened the gate for her to slip out, then latched it behind her. "Where's my Little Bit? I thought I'd find her strapped to your back." He held out a hand, and she slipped hers into his. He wove their fingers together. The perfect fit.

"Sleeping. Emma promised to call when she wakes."

The way Moriah tucked herself close to him made him wonder why he'd spent all week notching logs and framing doors instead of by this woman's side.

"Does that mean you have time for a walk? There's not much wind right now." As much as he dreaded the thought, there was a conversation they needed to have. His conscience wouldn't let him put if off much longer.

She studied his face for a moment, maybe hearing something in his tone that gave her pause. He tried to offer a casual smile as they stepped out of the barn.

"All right." Her voice sounded unsure, but at least she'd agreed.

They walked for a few minutes in silence, the warm sun taking away a little of winter's bite. Thankfully, the rays weren't bright enough to make his eyes sting.

Moriah was the first to break the quiet. "Rachel said Seth plans to ask Father Bergeron to come next Sunday to marry them."

That pang touched his chest again, but not so sharp as before. "That's what I hear." He could feel her gaze on him, but knew if he looked at her, she'd be able to read his thoughts.

"It's hard, isn't it?" Her gloved thumb stoked the back of his hand.

Apparently she could read his thoughts without seeing them in his eyes. He inhaled, then released a sigh. "Seth and I have always done things together. I guess I feel like I'm losing him."

She was quiet for another few strides, then her voice seemed hesitant as she spoke. "Do you plan to build your own cabin here?"

His gut squeezed. Now was the time to make good on his promise. He inhaled a breath and looked at her. "I didn't really have plans before, but I made you a promise I'll still keep."

She stopped walking and turned to meet his gaze, a glimpse of her old emotionless expression hovering on her face. "Which is?"

"I'll find your people, Moriah. Just like I said I would. But there's something I need to ask of you."

"Yes?" Still no expression on her face. That couldn't be good.

He squeezed her hand, gentling his voice and adding a note of pleading. "Stay here with my family until I come back. Don't bring her on the trail again. Please. I promise I'll search until I find them. I won't give up. But I couldn't stand it if something happened to either of you. I can't protect you in the wilderness like I need to." His chest ached as he waited for her response.

She looked away, into the distance, her mind somewhere far distant. Her throat worked, and he searched for some idea of her thoughts.

At last, she turned to face him, and something in her eyes looked almost like the glimmer of tears. "And after you find my people, what will you do? Come back and take Cherry and me to live with them?"

What was she asking? Hadn't that been her goal from the very beginning? He certainly didn't *want* to send her and the baby away. In fact, if that's where she wanted to live, he'd take up residence with her people, too.

A desperation welled up inside him, a feeling he'd been tamping down for a week now. Longer, really.

He took her other hand and faced her fully. It was time to tell everything, whether she was ready to hear it or not.

"Moriah, I haven't said anything because I know it's too soon. You're probably still—I mean, I *know* you're still grieving Henry. But I can't keep this from you any longer. I don't want there to be secrets or things unsaid between us."

He kept on before he lost his nerve. "I love you, Moriah. And I can't let you and Cherry ride away. I'll find your people, and if that's where you want to live, that's where I want to be, too. By your side as your husband. Loving you both." He raised one of her hands to his lips and pressed a kiss as he searched her eyes for some kind of response.

Her expression was unreadable for a long moment, and his heart felt like it might beat out of his chest. Then her eyes turned glassy. Tears? Maybe he should have waited to say all this until she'd had more time to grow accustomed to this place, to him. More time to grieve. Seven months couldn't be nearly long enough.

When she finally opened her mouth to speak, her lips parted for a long moment before words actually came out. He steeled himself, prepared his response. He would tell her they didn't have to talk about this now. In a few months, when she was ready, they could discuss the future.

In the meantime, he could keep himself occupied riding the countryside searching for a missing band of Piegan.

"Are you certain?"

Her words brought a flash of confusion, as quickly as his thoughts were spinning.

He replayed his declaration through his mind. She was asking if he was sure he loved her and wanted to marry her? He raised her other hand and kissed the fingers as he caught her gaze and held it. "I've never been more sure of anything. I'll wait as long as you need. Whenever you're ready, I'll be here."

Her chin trembled, and the sight pressed hard on his chest. *Lord, please don't let her cry. I'm not trying to push too hard. Should I have kept this all to myself?*

She squeezed his hands, and with a shaky breath, she nodded. "I love you, too. I never thought I could, but you're not like any person I've ever known—white or Indian."

Her words slipped inside him like a breath of clean, crisp air, clearing away all his worries. "Really?" His chest felt like it might inflate right out of his body.

A tear leaked from one of her eyes even as a radiant smile took over her face. She nodded. "Really."

He couldn't stand it a second longer. He released her hands and wrapped his arms around her, squeezing her as tight as he dared. Yet it didn't come close to expressing the pure joy sluicing through him. "Moriah." Her name felt like heaven on his lips.

She held him tightly, too, and for a long moment they stood like that. He breathed in her sweet scent, resting his cheek on her silky hair.

Then she pulled back enough to look up into his face. "Don't leave us this winter. Now that I have you, it's not so urgent to find my people."

He studied her face for signs of longing. She'd been so hurt when they'd found that empty valley, as though she'd been abandoned. Was it really only the safety of the group she'd longed for? He couldn't let her give this up if she really wanted it. "Shall I go when the weather warms then?"

She reached up to press a hand to his chest. "One day I'd like to see them again. I miss my mother and grandfather. Even my half-brothers and sisters. But we'll find them when the time comes. For now, we have a life to make here."

Could it be possible she really felt that way? He wanted to squeeze his eyes shut and break out in a psalm of praise. *Thank you, Father. Your grace overflows so much more than I deserve.*

He moved his hands up and cupped her face in both his palms, then lowered his mouth to brush a kiss on her lips. He kept it to a single caress, then raised his head to look in her eyes again. "Moriah Clark, you're so much more than I ever dreamed of. I love you."

She reached a hand behind his neck and pulled his mouth back down to hers. And this time, he let his kiss say all that was in his heart.

EPILOGUE

*S*amuel stared out the bedchamber window at the fresh-hewn logs of the two cabins positioned along the edge of the valley. It was hard to believe only a couple weeks ago, one of those structures had been nothing more than a thought.

And now it was his own cabin. The home he would share with Moriah and Cherry, and all the babies God blessed them with in the future.

When they'd told Seth and the rest of the family their news, his impulsive twin brother had insisted they set right to work on the cabin for Samuel and Moriah.

Rachel had even offered to postpone their own ceremony until the second home could be built, to allow for a double wedding. And he couldn't deny that sharing this special day with his twin felt right.

Moriah seemed to like the notion, so they'd agreed, and the resulting two weeks were a blur of long hours felling trees, notching logs, mounting door frames, and a long list of other tasks. Neither cabin held furniture yet, except the mattress ticks the women had sewn and a few other small things donated from family members, but at least the homes were dry and warm with fires laid in each hearth.

Now, the wedding day had arrived.

Was he doing the right thing rushing into this marriage with Moriah? He was certain beyond a shadow of doubt she was the woman God planned for him, but did she need more time before the wedding?

He wanted no regrets as they entered this new phase of their lives.

She said she was ready. Had given no sign of hesitation. But he didn't want her to feel rushed. *Is this right, Lord? Show me a sign, or give me peace, if this is Your will.*

Was he willing to postpone things if the Lord didn't provide either of those requests? *Help me do the right thing.*

"Having second thoughts?" Seth's voice turned him from the window.

His brother was looking dapper for the occasion, with hair neatly trimmed and a fresh shave.

Samuel shook his head. "Not about marrying her. But I wonder if I'm rushing her too much. I don't want her to have regrets."

Seth's brow wrinkled as he slowly nodded. "I know what you mean. Think you should go talk to her?"

"Wouldn't be easy with Emma standing guard." Their sister-in-law had gathered Rachel and Moriah into her house early that morning and given strict instructions neither of the men was to attempt contact before the ceremony. Something about seeing the bride before the wedding being against tradition.

He could figure out a way past her if he really did need to speak with Moriah, and maybe he should.

A soft step sounded outside the bedchamber door, then a knock. "You boys decent?"

Noelle. Seth reached back and opened the door for their sister.

Her face shone in a bright smile, with just a hint of the sass that was Noelle. "I came to make sure you boys are fixed up properly, and I also have messages from your ladies."

She stepped into the room and handed Seth a note, then moved forward to Samuel. She stopped just before him, and her face grew earnest as she locked gazes with him. "She wanted me to tell you she's ready. She could never be more ready than she is now."

Samuel sucked in a breath. Really? His eyes drifted closed as a wash of relief swept all the way through him. *Thank you, Lord.*

Noelle gripped his arm, pulling his eyes open and his focus back to her. "You're going to be happy, little brother." Her mouth pulled in a trembling smile, then she slipped into his arms and wrapped herself around him.

He held her tight, until—with a sniff—she pulled away and turned to Seth. "You, too."

She stepped into Seth's arms, and he returned the hug, pressing a kiss to her hair, then meeting Samuel's gaze over the top of her head. He wore a grin that matched the joy in Samuel's own chest.

Today would be the best day ever.

~

"They're here."

Moriah turned from her daughter to see Emma, who'd just slipped into the bedchamber and closed the door behind her.

"Anything you ladies need?" She walked first to Rachel, who stood in front of the mirror, fussing with her hair again. Emma stopped behind the other woman and studied the mirror, then tucked a strand of Rachel's honey blonde hair. "Lovely." She squeezed Rachel's arms and the two shared a smile in the mirror.

Then Emma turned toward the bed, where Moriah sat bouncing Cherry in her lap. Moriah tried to offer a confident smile, but she wasn't sure she accomplished it.

Emma came to sit on the bed beside her and slipped an arm around her shoulders. "I couldn't be happier you ladies are joining the family. I know your homes aren't quite set-up the way you'll want them, but we'll remedy that over the next few weeks. Today is our day to celebrate."

Moriah inhaled a breath. Yes. She was celebrating inside, yet she'd never had such a fuss made over her. She'd feel more like herself when she was with Samuel again.

Rachel turned from the mirror with a radiant smile. "I'm ready when you are, Moriah."

She summoned a nod. "Me, too."

Emma helped her stand, which was good because her legs were a little wobbly at first.

"Ready for me to take her?" Emma reached for the baby.

Moriah pressed a final kiss to her daughter's head, then whispered in her tiny ear, "Here we go."

Cherry went easily to this woman she'd come to know well in the past weeks, and Emma led the way to the door. When she pulled it open, the low hum of voices in the outer room stilled. She stepped through the doorway. "We're ready." Her smile sounded bright in the announcement, although Moriah couldn't see her face.

A hand slipped around Moriah's arm, and she turned to look at Rachel. She searched her sister-in-law's eyes for hesitation or remorse, but saw nothing there except earnest joy.

"I'm so glad to be sharing today with you, Moriah. I think this makes us doubly sisters, right?" No censure, only acceptance in the words and in her smile.

A happy ache tightened in Moriah's chest, and the sting of tears burned her eyes. She'd never felt so much a part, so loved, as these past few weeks. She nodded. "Sisters. Doubly."

Rachel pulled her close for a sideways hug, then they both straightened and stepped forward through the door.

A room full of people awaited, but it didn't take long for her gaze to find Samuel. His rich brown eyes were locked on her, and the love reflected there warmed her with every step she took across the room.

She reached Samuel's side and slipped her hand into his, and as they turned to face Father Bergeron, the rightness of the moment settled over her once more. *Thank you, Lord, for providing for me even when I didn't know what I needed.*

That desperate prayer she'd prayed all those weeks ago, as she was under siege and struggling to keep herself and the baby alive, had been answered in ways she'd never imagined.

Now with this man at her side, she was ready to step into whatever new blessings the Father had in store for them.

And she had a feeling the adventure had only just begun.

Did you enjoy Samuel and Moriah's story? I hope so!
Would you take a quick minute to leave a review?
It doesn't have to be long. Just a sentence or two telling what you liked about the story!

~

And would you like to receive a **free short story about a special moment in Gideon and Leah's happily-ever after**?
Get the free short story and sign-up for insider email updates at https://mistymbeller.com/free-short-story

And here's a peek at the next book in the series, *This Healing Journey*, (Hannah's story! Remember the baby born to Simeon and Emma?):

CHAPTER ONE

On the brink of finally claiming this dream. Why do my fears rise to taunt me now?

~ Nathaniel

JUNE, 1880
NEAR BUTTE, MONTANA TERRITORY

Meeting a stranger shouldn't make him so nervous. Shouldn't even give him a second's worry. Nathaniel Peak rubbed a sweating palm down his trouser leg as he tried to settle into his horse's stride. After all, he'd faced down hundreds of enemy rifles and charged into the midst of Indian war cries and brutal spears. By the grace of God he'd survived, and finally escaped the ruthless life in the cavalry he'd grown to hate so fiercely.

Now, a simple life as a civilian rancher shouldn't set his nerves on edge. He was only meeting a neighbor. Maybe a family. These were the people living nearest his new homestead. The neighbors he could call on for help, and return the favor in kind.

Yet, since the rising sun had awakened him this morning, he'd had a gnawing in his gut. The feeling that came before battle, the sting of goose flesh and hair standing on end. But why?

It wasn't as if these landowners were more important than others he'd met in his life. He was making too much of this introduction in his mind, but he couldn't seem to squelch the anxiety.

To his left, the trees parted to reveal a majestic view of distant mountain peaks rising up as far as he could see. *This* was why he'd chosen to start his ranch here. Views like that stirred something deep inside him, making him come alive in a way he wanted to feel for the rest of his days.

To the right, a worn path turned off the main trail and he reined his mare that direction, toward the spire of smoke rising above the trees. Would these be a pair of grizzled mountain men who'd teamed up to make their work a bit easier for themselves? Or a young couple trying to make a go of life in these majestic mountains, where a man could work his own land and appreciate the fruits of his labors?

As the trees gave way to an open clearing, the cabin sitting in the middle proved to be the source of the rising chimney smoke. A dog barked, then bounded from the porch toward him. A big white wooly animal who showed a pair of snarling teeth as it neared.

"Hey, there." He kept his horse moving forward steadily, careful to make sure his posture didn't show any hint of threat toward the canine. Nor any fear.

A sound from the cabin porch brought his focus up to where a man stepped outside. He paused at the top of the stairs, a hat shadowing his face so it was hard to get a read on his age and demeanor. The dog loped back to the porch and took its position beside the man.

Nathaniel stopped his horse about fifteen strides away the structure. Near enough they could speak without yelling, but far enough he didn't appear to be pushing his way in uninvited.

He raised a hand. "Howdy."

The other man nodded, lifting a matching palm in greeting. "We don't see many new faces around here." His voice sounded friendly enough.

Nathaniel forced away a bit of his nerves as he tipped up the brim of his hat so the fellow could get a clear look at him. "I'm home-steading the land to the east of you." He pointed in the direction of his property. "There's an old trapper's cabin I've been staying in. Maybe you've seen the place. Anyway, thought I'd come introduce myself. Nathaniel Peak."

"Glad to meet you." The man stepped down the stairs and moved toward him. "I'm Reuben Scott. Come in and stay a bit. My wife'll have coffee on and biscuits made fresh this morning."

Nathaniel eased out a breath as he dismounted. He turned to Scott and extended a hand to meet the outstretched grip. "I'd appreciate that." This was almost better than he could have hoped. He could address business now without having to come back a second time.

He tied his horse at the hitching post to the right of the stairs, then fell into step beside Reuben Scott, glancing around the clearing at the barn, corrals, and a few other outbuildings. "Looks like a nice place you have here."

Not luxurious, to be sure, but well-equipped for a quiet mountain ranch. It would take some doing to get his own cluster of ramshackle buildings up to this level of simple efficiency. All the structures here seemed well-maintained.

On the porch, Scott motioned to the dog to stay out, then pushed open the door and stepped inside first. "We've a visitor." His words were directed to someone within, then he cleared the opening and waved for Nathaniel to enter.

As he stepped into the interior, he squinted to catch the surround-ings while his eyes adjusted to the dimmer lighting. Sound to his right drew his focus.

A woman stood over a cookstove, a table to her back. She replaced the lid on a pot and turned to him with a smile. "Welcome."

Reuben Scott moved near her, then pointed to Nathaniel. "This is our new neighbor to the east, Nathaniel Peak. He's taken the old hunting cabin."

She clasped her hands together as joy lit her pretty face. "Wonderful. I'm Cathleen Scott." She motioned toward the table. "Sit and visit. I'll pour coffee."

Either these two were starved for human interaction, or they were genuinely pleasant people. Whichever the case, he stepped toward the table and sank into a ladder-back chair on the long side. Reuben took one at the head.

"Are you new to the area?" The man leaned back in his seat, crossing his arms in a comfortable pose.

"Mostly. I just finished four years in the 2nd US Calvary Regiment, B Troop. We rode through here a couple times, and I remembered it being one of the prettiest countries I'd ever seen. As soon as I could get away from the fighting, I made my way back."

He watched Reuben's face as he spoke, and didn't miss the way his eyes seemed to close off, although his expression didn't harden. Did this man feel the same way about the Indian wars? Or did he have another reason to dislike the cavalry?

Mrs. Scott placed mugs in front of each of them—ceramic, not the tin he was so accustomed to. He glanced at her face, but saw nothing there except kind civility.

Perhaps this was a good time to ease the conversation away from himself. Turning back to the man, he took a sip of the warm brew. The liquid eased down without a hint of bitterness. "Ah, that's good. Shouldn't even carry the same name as the sludge we drank in the regiment."

Reuben's jaw tightened at the word *regiment*. The man clearly disliked something about the cavalry—a sentiment Nathaniel shared with him. Maybe if he told of his reasons for leaving, they could find common ground with better footing.

He set the mug on the table and met the man's gaze. "I signed on to the cavalry back in Virginia, the same as my father had done, and his father before him. It was my mother's greatest wish that I follow in their footsteps and protect my country on horseback. Within days, I was assigned to the 2nd Regiment and sent westward with a group of other new troopers. What I found when I arrived was nothing like what I expected."

He stared into his mug as those early days came back to him. "The Indians. I..." How did he say this without seeming overly harsh toward his superiors? Not all had been heartless. For many, this was simply a war they'd been commanded to win. Yet war should never be waged against women and children.

Swallowing, he did his best to sum up the story in as few words as possible. "I suppose you could say I didn't always agree with the methods we were commanded to use in fulfilling our orders. For that matter, I struggled with why there was such a need to keep the Indians confined to reservations in the first place. In many ways, it seems possible and better for us all to settle in together doing what the Bible says. 'As much as possible, live peaceably with all men.'" He scrubbed a hand through his hair. "I suppose soldiering wasn't the best line of work for me."

He chanced a look at Reuben. He'd never bared his soul so thoroughly to strangers. What would the man say? He'd not meant to put him on the spot, nor dive into such weighty matters in the first five minutes of conversation. Perhaps it was best they change the subject now.

Reuben's jaw had softened, and his mouth curved in a hint of a smile. "I couldn't have said it better myself. The part about living peaceably that is." Then he reached a hand forward. It took Nathaniel a second for his stunned mind to realize what the man offered.

He took the extended hand, accepting the friendship locked firmly in the grip. Reuben's gaze settled in his, something like respect shimmering in his dark eyes.

Then the man eased back in his chair with a comfortable sigh. "Now tell us, what do you need to help you settle in? That shack's not been lived in regularly for a while that I know of. You need a hand to make the place habitable?"

Mrs. Scott placed a plate of fluffy biscuits on the table, along with butter and some kind of jam. He'd meant only a glance at the food, but the aroma didn't do the fare justice. He could almost taste the warm melding of sweet flavors, even though it had been years since he'd enjoyed such bliss. Not since he joined the cavalry.

A chuckle drifted from Reuben as the man nudged the plate toward him. "Go ahead. Eat. Cathleen makes better biscuits than anyone I know. Even better than my mum's."

"Speaking of Mum, I think I hear her waking." Mrs. Scott spoke for the first time since they'd sat at the table. The swish of her skirts sounded as she moved toward the doors against the back wall.

Reuben watched his wife go, a glimmer in his eyes most married men seemed to lose after the courting days. Then he turned his focus back to Nathaniel. "Mum doesn't always remember much these days. It might confuse her to meet you. She'll be polite, but she may think you're someone she once knew."

Nathaniel nodded. "Getting old isn't easy." He couldn't withstand the call of the biscuits any longer, but tried not to make a fanfare of scooping one onto his plate.

Reuben did the same, and an easy quiet settled as they loaded the bread with extras. The first bite was heavenly, even better than he'd imagined.

"So you didn't say how we could help. I'm sure Cathy will want to send food with you."

As welcome as the words were, they invaded Nathaniel's moment of pleasure like a buzzing horsefly in summer's heat. Still, he pulled himself back to his main purpose for coming here.

"Actually, I'm looking to buy stock. Cattle and good horseflesh if I can find it. My plan is to raise mostly horses, but the cattle will help offset the lean times. Do you know the best places in this area to buy healthy animals?"

Reuben's gaze drifted into the distance as he chewed, his mind likely far away. "I don't mind selling you a few of our cattle, but our herd's still low from when I had to trade some to O'Hennessey last year. He may have more to part with than we do. I know he has a few horses, but I'm not sure if any will be what you're looking for." He turned back to Nathaniel. "He's our neighbor to the west, about an hour's ride. I can go over there with you if you'd like."

Nathaniel tried to keep the grin from spreading too wide on his face. "I'd appreciate that."

A clanging sounded from the back chamber. And at the same time the dog growled on the porch outside. Reuben's head cocked, then he pushed to his feet and moved toward the small window at the far end of the room.

Nathaniel stood, too. Had someone else come to visit? He wouldn't expect many people this far up in the mountains. Reuben's face looked troubled as he peered through the glass, then he stepped to the rear door his wife had entered. When he poked his head inside what must be a bed chamber, the hum of voices sounded, but not loud enough for Nathaniel to make out words.

He kept his place by the table, waiting to see where he was needed. Reuben strode toward the front door, then paused as if just remembering Nathaniel was there. He waved toward the porch. "Three unfamiliar riders. You can come meet them too. Maybe we have more new neighbors."

Nathaniel followed him out, but couldn't summon the light spirit the man's words tried to relay. Maybe because Reuben's face held a seriousness that matched the foreboding in his own chest.

Get THIS HEALING JOURNEY at your favorite retailer.

ABOUT THE AUTHOR

 **Misty M. Beller** is a *USA Today* bestselling author of romantic mountain stories, set on the 1800s frontier and woven with the truth of God's love.

Raised on a farm and surrounded by family, Misty developed her love for horses, history, and adventure. These days, her husband and children provide fresh adventure every day, keeping her both grounded and crazy.

Misty's passion is to create inspiring Christian fiction infused with the grandeur of the mountains, writing historical romance that displays God's abundant love through the twists and turns in the lives of her characters.

Sharing her stories with readers is a dream come true for Misty. She writes from her country home in South Carolina and escapes to the mountains any chance she gets.

Connect with Misty at www.MistyMBeller.com

ALSO BY MISTY M. BELLER

Call of the Rockies

Freedom in the Mountain Wind

Hope in the Mountain River

Light in the Mountain Sky

Courage in the Mountain Wilderness

Faith in the Mountain Valley

Honor in the Mountain Refuge

Peace in the Mountain Haven

Calm in the Mountain Storm

Brides of Laurent

A Warrior's Heart

A Healer's Promise

A Daughter's Courage

Hearts of Montana

Hope's Highest Mountain

Love's Mountain Quest

Faith's Mountain Home

Texas Rancher Trilogy

The Rancher Takes a Cook

The Ranger Takes a Bride

The Rancher Takes a Cowgirl

Wyoming Mountain Tales

A Pony Express Romance

A Rocky Mountain Romance

A Sweetwater River Romance

A Mountain Christmas Romance

The Mountain Series

The Lady and the Mountain Man

The Lady and the Mountain Doctor

The Lady and the Mountain Fire

The Lady and the Mountain Promise

The Lady and the Mountain Call

This Treacherous Journey

This Wilderness Journey

This Freedom Journey (novella)

This Courageous Journey

This Homeward Journey

This Daring Journey

This Healing Journey